KATHI S. BARTON

were going to be tried for attempted murder as well as damage to the school. It didn't seem like much, the damage part, but it had taken the better part of a week to get the blood out of the vestibule where they'd been caught. Shaller and Duncan had each been shot four times by the officers who were first on the scene.

"Mom wants you to go see her when you have a chance." He just nodded at Alaric. "She said that you've been avoiding her, and she's not happy. And when Mom isn't happy, no one is. So make sure you go and see her."

"I will. I will." He would, too, because he loved his mom and would move heaven and earth for her. "Why didn't she just call me and tell me? Or is she not talking to me either?"

"I don't know. I'm just the messenger, don't get pissy with me." Alaric, another brother and officer of the law, stretched his neck so that it popped. "Aaron is the one who is upset with you, and I don't blame him. The things you spouted off were just stupid, and I hope when your mate comes around, he can be there to tell you he told you so. You're stupid for thinking that you can simply avoid everyone and that will make it work. Do you remember how Aaron found Mac? She fell into his lap when he was coming out of the building."

"I heard the story a dozen times. And I'm sick of it. I'm sick of everyone telling me how stupid I'm being, too. I know what I want, and none of you is going to talk me into anything different. I don't want a mate, and if she does just fall in my lap like Mac did, then she's going to have to learn some lessons that I don't mind teaching her." He asked him what that was supposed to mean. "That's between me and her. But I'm not going to be taking a mate. I have no wish to be with the same woman all the time when there are so many out there to have. Mark my words, I'm going to be the only one that doesn't have to look to where his life has gone twenty or so years from now."

"Whatever. You go on believing that you're going to have the perfect life without a mate. I'm going to laugh my ass off when she comes around, too. I might even have to tell her what a jerk you've been about her, too." Alaric laughed like he'd been told the best joke. "Yes, sir. I'm going to have a blast laughing at you trying to get on her good side when you've fucked up badly with her."

"Don't hold your breath on it." He went back to the paperwork that he'd left this morning to catch a shoplifter. As soon as he was finished with it, he had to file the things that he'd been working on. He hated filing shit. It was a job that he would avoid so much that he'd have a month's worth of reports on his desk before he got around to filing them in the proper places.

It was nearly quitting time when he realized

that he'd not called his mom yet. She'd be upset with him, but he knew that she loved him. As soon as he clocked out, he made his way home and bumped into Mac as she was coming out the door. He'd forgotten that she and Aaron lived in the big house with their parents.

"Your mom is looking for you." He told her that he'd been told. "Don't get snippy with me, you little pisser. I'll take you to task, and you won't like that anymore than you want a mate. I'm not one of your buddies at work."

"I'm sorry. It's been a long day. I had to file paperwork all afternoon, and I'm grumpy." He moved past her into the house and found his mom in the kitchen with Aaron. As soon as he walked in, Aaron stood up and left. It was going to be like that for a long time if he didn't get his head out of his ass soon. Zeno knew what he was doing, and the sooner that he got on board with it, the better things would be. "Hello, Mom. I haven't been avoiding you. I've just been busy."

"I'm sure you haven't been. What's this I hear about you not wanting a mate?" He looked at his brother and glared. "He didn't tell me. I heard it through your grandda. He told me that you were out there asking about how to avoid having a mate and what to do about it if she came into your life. You can't be seriously thinking that you can just stop seeing women and that will be the end of it. Do you remember how Mac came into Aaron's life?"

"Yes. Christ, will everyone just get off my back?" He knew the moment that the words left his mouth, he was in trouble. The slap to his face from his mom hurt, but it was Aaron jerking him up from the chair that scared him a bit. Aaron was bigger than him by a lot. And meaner too. He'd seen it. "I didn't mean to say that."

"You're telling the wrong person." He looked at his mom, who was crying, and his heart broke. "See what you did? Do you want me to kick your ass? I will for no other reason than you making Mom cry. What's wrong with you?"

The shake to his body made him slightly ill. But he wasn't going to allow his big brother to take him to task any more than he would his parents. When he was slammed back in the chair, he took his mom's hand into his. "I'm so sorry, Mom. I've had a really crappy day, and I didn't mean to take it out on you. I'm profoundly sorry for what I said. Please forgive me."

"What is wrong with you lately?" He said that everyone was on him for having an opinion about having a mate. "Well, I'm none too happy with you either. To think those things is just wrong, son. You have to know that."

"I just don't want someone tying me down. I

want to have the same life as I have now. Free to come and go as I please and do what I wanted." She pulled her hand from his when she stood up and patted Aaron on the chest. "He told you and not grandda, didn't he? Running to you to get me into trouble. It sounds like something that he'd do."

"I want you to leave this house right now, Zeno. I don't have to put up with your painful words, and I'm not." She moved to the kitchen door and opened it. "Get out now before you say something that you're going to regret. I told you where I got my information, and I can't lie to you. You've hurt me enough, and I think it's time that you were going."

"Mom, I'm sorry." When she lifted her chin up, he could see the tears rolling down her cheeks. "I'm so sorry, Mom, but this is something that I've given a great deal of thought to. I should be able to have my own opinion."

"It's not your opinion that has this family upset with you. It's the way you've been treating everyone. Snipping and snapping at people just because you don't want a mate. Well, that's fine, and I hope someday someone comes into your life and makes you see reason. However, I hope that she tears you up inside as you've done to me. I'm heartbroken that you would even think to talk to me like you have." He asked her when he'd talked to her badly. "Saturday night at dinner. You made a harsh comment about me cooking dinner. Then you tried to blow it off like it was nothing more than a joke. It hurt me that you think that I don't have anything to do with cooking the meal that brings you home on Saturday. I do it all. I just don't clean up. And you'd know that if you came around more. I think that it's time that you left. I've had my heart broken by you enough for one week."

He left, but he wasn't happy about it. They were all making him out to be the bad guy, and he wasn't. It was none of their business that he didn't want a mate, and they should have respected him for that. But no, they'd rather blame it all on him, like he wasn't the one who was being persecuted for what he'd said. When they all found their mates, he was the only one who was going to be happy, and he'd show them then. There was no way he was going to find his mate now, even if she were to fall in his lap as Mac did to Aaron. He was made of sterner stuff than that.

~*~

Shawn was having a hard time finding his brother. He knew that he had a cell phone on him, but either he had not paid the bill or he was avoiding him. It had to be the bill, as there was no way that he'd think he'd be all right with being avoided. He was going to find him even if he had to go to the morgue to do so. And he'd better be dead if he knew the mess that he'd been trying to find him in.

"I'm looking for a man by the name of Benjamin Troff. He'd be about my height and a little skinnier." He was at the last police station in the county, and he wasn't having any luck. When the man told him to wait a moment, he stood there and had himself a look around. It was like all the other station houses that he'd been in. Dark and in need of a little color. When the man came back, he was ready to ask him where else he could be when he smiled.

"He's been arrested. A month ago now. Since he can't make bail, he's been sitting in the cell waiting for his turn with the judge." He asked what he'd done. "He threatened an FBI agent. Well, two of them. And they pressed charges against him. He's been a model convict. He even says please and thank you when he gets his dinner."

"Who is it I have to kill to get him out of jail?" He was serious, so he was startled when the officer laughed. "I want my brother out of jail right now. He came here to get money from our sister, and that was the last time I heard from him."

"That's who he threatened. Your sister and another agent." His sister was an FBI agent? He must have heard him wrong. "No, they're both agents. Though now I think that Mac has been teaching over at the elementary school for a while now. They were short-staffed when she said that she could do it. Did you know that she minored in elementary teaching when she went to college?"

"I didn't know she was smart enough to go to college. You have to be shitting me about her becoming an agent. There is no way that I'd allow that, and she has to know it." He asked him if he knew she was over eighteen. "Of course, I know that moron. But that don't give her any reason to become an agent. Where is she anyway?"

"I would tone it down if I were you. We don't take too well to being called names when we're on duty." He just laughed and shook his head. "I don't know where Mac is, but your brother is back in the cells. He'll be there until at least a week from Monday. He'll be able to see the judge then. If you want to see him, you're going to have to leave your personal items here at the desk. And that would include any knives you have on yourself."

After leaving his personal items with the officer, he was taken back to see his brother. He was ready to bitch at him for being caught when he got a good look at him. Christ, what were they doing to him while he was locked up? Starve him? Benjamin looked like he'd lost thirty pounds, weight that he couldn't afford to lose.

"What's happened to you? Are they not feeding

you?" He said that he was glad to see him, too. "I'm serious. You look like shit. Are they starving you for sure?"

"I'm just eating better. And they let me walk around with an officer outside when the weather is good. It's good for me. Where have you been?" He said he'd been looking for him. "I've been here all along. I couldn't call you on account of them not letting me use my cell phone. It's probably dead by now. Anyway, I came here to get money from Mac and ran into some trouble. She's a Federal officer now. Did you know that? Don't threaten her or you'll be in the cell next to mine."

"I'll do what I want to her, and you should know that. Christ, I can't believe how skinny you look. You haven't been eating well at all, have you?" He said that he doesn't eat fast food anymore, but healthy food. "Why would you go and do something like that? Fast food is the food of the gods if you ask me."

"It's not like I can go out and get me some now, can I?" When he finally stood up, he could see that he really wasn't all that skinny but healthier looking. "I've been debating on telling you this or not, but don't go trying to get anything from Mac. She's more than likely married by now and has a shifter for a husband. Big mother fucking tiger that nearly killed me when I tried to get some cash from her. Look what he did to me and my body."

He put out his hand, and he couldn't believe the nasty scar that was there. It was five stabs that looked like they'd gone clean through his hand. Then, when he removed his shirt, he could see the same marks on his chest. Like the tiger had been on top of him, smashing him into the dirt.

"I was lucky. People said that because he didn't kill me when I tried to get Mac to do something she didn't want to. All I wanted was a couple of thousand dollars, but she wasn't having it. Told me right off she wasn't going to be paying me for the rest of her life. How do you suppose she knew that I'd be coming by often to get a couple grand more?" He laughed. "I started out wanting ten grand. I was going to share it with you and Dad, but by the end, I was begging for anything that they could give me. I was stupid for thinking that I could take on a tiger and come out on top."

"I'm not afraid of a tiger shifter. They're all pussies." Benjamin said that this man wasn't. "So what. I'm going to take her to task, too, on you being hurt. Did she do anything to keep you from being clawed like you are?"

"No. But I think she had a lot to do with me not being dead. I'm just saying, Shawn, you'd be better off robbing a bank than to fuck with Mac. She'll get you killed as soon as you try anything with her. I'm not shitting you right now." He said he wasn't afraid. "Then you have a nice short life. I don't think he's going to take too kindly to two of us wanting the same thing from her. I'm done. I learned my lesson right away. If you don't heed my words, I don't know what to tell you."

"You will be all right when I get you out of here. She'll be paying for an operation, too, that will take care of those scars. Also, I'm going to be asking for more than two grand. I want some pocket money to flash around, and she's going to be giving it to me." Benjamin told him good luck. "It's not luck that I need. I'm meaner than he is, and I'm going to get what I want. See that I don't."

"I don't want to see you dead, but if you're set on doing this, you go right ahead. I did warn you." He went to the cot and sat back down. "What've you been up to? I've been reading while stuck in here, and I'm enjoying myself. It's been a long time since I've had some time to myself, and I'd forgotten how much I enjoy it. How's Dad? I've not heard from him either."

"Dad was in prison too the last time I saw him, should be getting out soon enough, then he'll come here. He'd been stealing cars off the street, and he got caught. He was doing it in his own town, and that's why they caught him. You should never steal where you sleep. It'll get you caught every time." Shaking his head, he couldn't believe that he had to tell his father that and said as much to his brother. "When he gets out, he's going to be none too happy to find out that you've been hurt by Mac. She's going to piss him off something terrible, and I don't blame him. Just look at you! You're nothing but skin and bones."

"I'm healthy. And I feel better, too." Telling his little brother that he just didn't know the difference between feeling good and being healthy. "Yes, I do. I told you that I feel better than I have in a long time. And when I get out of here, I'm going to be following the rules too. I saw my life flashing before my eyes when they couldn't get my wounds to close up, and I'm not going to get myself in that way again. I had to tell him I was sorry. Both of them and mean it too. I did and finally stopped bleeding my life away."

"You're full of shit." Benjamin just waved him off like he knew better. Well, he was older and did know better. "When you get out of here, and there aren't any more cops watching you, you'll change back to what you were doing before. And I'll be there telling you how proud I am of you, too. You'll see. Mark my words, they're killing you here, and that's about the truth of it."

"There was never any talking to you when you got something into your head. I'm doing fine and will continue to do fine right up until I meet my maker. You'll just have to go on without me. I'm happy to be doing what I'm doing." Shawn couldn't believe that this was his brother talking and decided they were feeding him something to be off his noodle. He told him that once he was away, he'd know. "I know already. I'm fine. But you had better listen to me and leave Mac and her husband alone. They'll kill you and not have a second glance at you when they do."

After leaving his brother, knowing that he was right, he went and found him a place to stay. He really couldn't afford anything right now, but he had a credit card that he'd stolen about a week ago and hoped that it would still be worth something. All he needed was to get into the hotel somewhere, and he'd have Mac picking up the tab. While he didn't know how much money she might have, he was going to take every penny of it. She didn't owe him, but that's what he was going to tell her. She owed him because he'd not killed her when she'd been a kid. That should be worth something to her, he thought with a grin.

The hotel didn't even blink an eye when he turned over his credit card. He hadn't really looked at it until he'd been handed it back, but it had the name of the woman on it that he'd killed a week ago. She might still be out in the field where he'd left her, and nobody knew about the cards yet.

He didn't get him the best room in the place, but a nice one. It had double beds for when his father came to town, so they could share. He'd be getting out of prison soon and would be hanging around him for a while. As excited as he was, he knew that his dad was going to be twice as excited because he had a place for him to stay. Usually, they stayed in something that was abandoned, without running water or heat. Now he had all the things that came with the hotel, and he was happy for it.

Unpacking his gear, he decided that he needed to put his guns up where the staff couldn't find them. That's all he needed was for some little bitch to find them and tell the police. They'd be happy to get them, was what he knew, because they'd be solving a few cases if they tried to fire them and compare bullets. He never got rid of a good gun.

He probably should have. Gotten rid of them as soon as they'd been used. Looking at his knife set, he was amazed at how clean it looked. But he'd seen enough shows and been around enough inmates that he knew no matter how clean they looked, the police would find a bit of blood on them that would jack you up for years. And his might well have a lot of little specs of blood from a lot of deaths.

If Shawn were caught again, he'd go in for life. That three-times-and-you're-done rule wouldn't even get him a good prison as he'd been in and out of the system five times. He just kept getting caught. But no more. He had rules that he followed, too, and that was keeping him not only under the radar but out of prison, too. He wasn't going back, even if he had to kill the entire department of men in blue to get away with something. And he'd do it too. There was no way he was going back to prison for life. Lifers in prison were the worst kind of inmates. They'd just as soon kill you as to look at you. What did they have to lose? Nothing. They were already in for their entire life.

Hiding his guns behind the big dresser, he looked around the room for a place to hide his knives. He wasn't going to put them with his guns because he carried them around with him all the time and needed them to be where he could get to them. There was no telling when he might need one of them to show a pussy what he was made of. And he wanted them on him when he met up with Mac. He might have to give her a few scars to show her what it was like.

Chapter 2

Zeno couldn't wrap his head around his mother kicking him out of the house. It wasn't fair that Aaron was the one who had started the trouble with him finding his mate. Well, that's not true; he'd not been responsible for his feelings on finding a mate. He'd had them for a while now, and he'd been keeping it to himself so that he'd not have the trouble that he was having now. He knew that they'd be pissed off. Just not as bad as he was having now.

Going back to the condo, he was ready to call it a day when his dad called. He knew that Mom would run to him about how he'd disrespected her. Not that he didn't deserve whatever his dad gave him. He hurt for hurting his mom and making her cry. But it was unfair of them to think that he needed to be on the same page as the rest of them were.

"What do you have to say for yourself?" He said he was sorry. "You're telling the wrong person that. I want to know what you said that made your mother cry. And she was still upset when she called me to tell me that she slapped you. If I had been there, you can bet your sweet ass it would have been much more than that."

"I'm sorry. I told Mom I was sorry too, but I can't let you guys run my life about this mate business." He said that he didn't care, but he should have chosen his words better. "You're right, I should have just kept my mouth shut on all of it."

"If that's the way you feel, then you have every right to feel that way. Don't go projecting onto others your opinions and anger when they don't agree with you. That's not the way we do things in our family." Had he done that? He wasn't sure, but he wasn't going to get into a fight with his dad. He had too much respect for him to do that. He should have had that much for his mom, too, but she'd hit him, and that wasn't right either.

They talked for another hour, with him listening mostly to his dad telling him what he needed to do before the grandparents found out. Grandda would be really upset, as he'd had his heart set on all of them making him a great grandda. If the others did it, then he'd be all right. He wondered if any of his brothers felt the same way he did about finding a mate.

It took him three hours to calm down enough that he was feeling better. He was going to have to talk to Aaron, too, he knew. And Mac. He wasn't looking forward to talking to either one of them, but he had to in order to make his dad and mom not be as upset with him anymore. He was more concerned with his parents being upset with him than he was his brother at this point. Aaron could be avoided until things settled down. He couldn't do anything that would make his parents hate him; they'd told him that all his life, but they could be disappointed in him, and he thought that hurt more. He'd never disappointed either of them in his entire life.

At midnight, he was headed to bed. He felt like shit, but he knew that he needed to sleep before he went to work in the morning. That was when he was planning on speaking to Aaron. He didn't want to, but knew that he'd have to talk to him sooner rather than later. He just hoped that they wouldn't come to blows. Aaron and himself were the most stubborn of the lot of them, and he knew that for a fact.

Getting up in the morning had been hard. He'd done a lot of soul searching while in bed, and he didn't think that he'd slept all that much. Now here he was on his way to work, and he just didn't have it in him to be apologetic. But he was going to try his damnest to make Aaron see things his way. He didn't have to agree with him, but he did want his idea on mates and marriage to be something that he acknowledged.

"Mom is still upset." He told his older brother that he was going to make it up to her. "I hope so. It's all right if you're mad at me. But she's Mom and doesn't deserve to be caught in the middle of things."

"No, you're right. I don't want you to be upset with me either, but you have to know that I didn't come to my decision easily. It's just something that I want." He nodded but didn't say anything. "Are you going to be mad at me for a while? I hope not. I love you."

"I love you too." He looked around the office, and Aaron asked him to come outside. He wanted to ask him if he was going to hurt him, but decided that, as a joke, it wouldn't go over all that well. "Let's not bring up our disagreement at work. I don't want anyone else knowing our business because it's none of their business."

"I agree. But I do want to talk to you. I never meant for us to—well, perhaps I did want to fight with you, but now I'm sorry." He told him it was all right. "No, it's not if you're going to be upset with me. And Mac. I really do love her, but what you two have I don't want. I don't want to be hanging onto one woman for the rest of my life."

"I know." Aaron didn't say anything when a couple of officers went into the building, passing right by them. "We'll just agree to disagree, and that'll be the end of it. If you ever find yourself with a woman who is your mate, come to me. I won't steer you wrong just because I don't agree with what you're saying."

"I shouldn't have pushed your buttons when I

was talking to you. I think I wanted you to fight me so that I could be right." He asked him what he thought he was right about. "I don't know. Women. I really do love all women, and the thought of being with just one is more than I want to admit right now. I don't think I'm going to change my mind about them either. I just can't see myself with one woman all the time. It's just not in me."

"All right. Like I said, we'll agree to disagree. You live that part of your life the way that you want, and I'll be in love with the greatest woman in the world." He smiled, and it looked sort of sappy on him. However, he didn't say anything, and that was good. They were talking, and that was more than he had this morning when he'd left the house. "Are you going to be over for dinner tomorrow night? Mom was planning a big meal that she said we'd all enjoy."

"I enjoy every meal that she makes. How will this one be any different?" He said he didn't know, but that was what she said. "Perhaps the grandparents can come over. They've not been to a Saturday night meal in a long time."

There was still tension between them, but they were working through it. He hoped in time they'd go back to being brothers like they'd been before, but it wasn't going to happen overnight. Aaron would have to see that he knew what he wanted and was going to get it. There would be no single woman in his life if he could help it. And he was going to try his damnest to not let one interfere in his life. He liked it just the way it was, where he was free to go as he pleased when he wished.

He went out on two calls before lunch, which had him doing more paperwork. That was the only part of his job that he didn't like, and that was something that he was going to have to get over. Filing paperwork was the worst part of it, but he'd have to get used to it if he wanted to become a detective like his brother. He didn't care if he became an FBI agent; he just wanted to be able to go out on calls like Aaron did sometimes.

After lunch, it was his turn to drive the cruiser between the schools. The high school would let out first, and that would be about two-fifteen. After that, the middle and grade school kids would be getting out, and that was when he had to be on his toes. The little ones sometimes forgot to look both ways when crossing the street, and he was at the crosswalk when they left. Most of the kids in town would have to walk to school. If they were within so many miles of the school, he thought that was good. But to have the little kids spread out all over town could be nerve-wracking.

Getting back to the stationhouse when his shift was over, he was ready for home. His not sleeping well last night was taking its toll on him; he just wanted to go to bed and not wake up until tomorrow. But duty called, and he was on call for the rest of the evening with one of the second shift people, and that wasn't so bad. He'd have to stay alert and not have a beer with his pizza. Not that he usually did, but he thought that he'd sleep better if he had a couple of sips of one.

Getting home with his pie, he sat down on the couch and had two slices before he changed out of his uniform. They'd been okayed to wear jeans with their shirts, and he was good with that. He could understand why Aaron was upset about the jogging pants. They were crappy-looking and didn't look as professional as the jeans did. He would have to tell Aaron he did a good thing about that, too. His brother was usually right.

After getting into his comfortable clothing, he sat down to the rest of his dinner. He could usually polish off an entire pizza by himself, but he was tired tonight and didn't have it in him to eat that much. Getting a shower after his dinner, he was ready for bed at seven-thirty and knew on some level that if he went to bed now, he'd never be able to sleep until morning. Then he'd be in the wrong cycle of things with work. Sometimes he hated not being able to sleep when things were weighing on his mind.

Turning on the television, he was glad to see that there were some ball games on. He didn't particularly care for baseball, but he'd watch it if there was nothing else on. When he realized that he'd not been paying attention, he finally went to bed. At nine-thirty, not only was he about asleep, but he also thought that he could sleep until morning and feel much better about his day.

When his alarm went off at seven, he was up and ready to go. He'd not realized how much he needed to sleep and to rest as he'd done last night. Feeling really good about himself, he not only ironed his shirt because he had time, but he also did a load of laundry so that he'd have clean clothing over the weekend.

Running the vacuum before he went into work, he was wondering how long it had been since he'd done that. And knew that it had to have been about a couple of weeks. He wasn't a slob or anything, but he did let the dusting go until it was really obvious that he'd not done it in a while.

When he got to work, it was his turn with the cruiser again. Making his rounds, he even stopped to get gas in it so that it would be full for the next shift. There was a lot to be said for a small-town police force, and he loved it here. Nothing really ever went on, and when it did, it was usually something that could be solved in a couple of days.

When Alaric came into the office to talk to him, the two of them went to lunch together. He loved the hot chicken sandwiches, so he got two of them, and Alaric did the same. They were on their second one each when he brought up that he was going to take the sergeant's exam soon, and he thought that he'd do pretty well on it.

"I've been studying for it for the past three months, and I think I'll do well on it. I don't think that I'll ace it or anything like that, but I know I'll do well enough to pass." He wished him luck. "How about you? You ever going to try and move up in the department? I'm thinking that you'd make a good chief. You seem to run the place as it is now. Except for Aaron. He's got things down pat and seems to be in a place where he wants to be."

"He's smart too, and that helps. And knowing the law like he does, it's small wonder that he'd not been asked to be the chief when Jamison leaves. You think that he'll be retiring soon? He seems to have the attitude that he's ready for it." He agreed with him, and they walked back to the station house. "I've been thinking about a lot of things lately, and I wonder if anything will come of it. There are a lot of things going on around town right now that I want to be involved in. I was thinking that if I didn't pass the sergeant's exam, I might run for mayor."

"You'd be good at that. I think that you'd do a better job than the one who is in office now. How long has he been running unopposed? Ten years at least." He said he thought it was about that. "We would have your back, too. And at least you'd have all of our votes as well." They both laughed, and he wanted to hug his brother but thought that he'd embarrass him. Thinking that he was going to do it anyway, Alaric hugged him. "That was well needed. Thank you."

"I needed it as well. I love you, Zeno. I don't say that often enough to any of you guys." He felt his eye fill and hugged his brother again. As soon as they parted ways, he knew that he was going to be happy for the rest of the day. If not forever. He was going to keep his opinions to himself about having a mate so that he didn't mess things up again. Going home, he decided to get his mom some roses and some chocolates. He knew that she would love them both because there was no occasion for them.

~*~

Peter wasn't going to be putting up with this shit for too much longer. His wife wasn't speaking to him, but that wasn't all that bad. But he couldn't get anyone to tell him why he'd been retired. He just wanted his job back so that he could knock some heads around. He didn't deserve to be treated this way.

"Your phone is ringing." He told his wife that he knew that when, in reality, he'd not heard it at all. When she huffed at him, he could have smacked the shit out of her, but didn't. She could be meaner than he could be when she was riled up. And he didn't want to have to deal with her too.

"I don't want to talk to anyone but my boss, and he's not returning my calls. I'm going to have to get drastic with him if he doesn't listen to reason."

He'd been made to retire when he'd demanded that a woman who had worked for him get her foot healed and get back to work. He knew that something was going on with the women who were being kidnapped, and his stepbrother, Larry Palmer, had his wife taken from him right under his nose. He wanted to get things investigated, but his hands were tied right now since he'd been forced out of his job. By God, he was going to have things go his way, or he was going to know the reason why.

"I'm not making supper tonight. I'm tired, and I don't want to have to mess with it when all you're going to do is complain about it." He asked her what he was supposed to do about his meal. "I don't care. I'm going to have myself a nice salad, and I know how you hate that, so you're going to be on your own."

"That's not the way things work for me. And you know it." She shrugged, and he again wanted to hit her. But he'd not. Not yet, anyway. "What am I supposed to do about eating? It's your job to make sure that I get my food on the table when I'm ready for it. What else do you have to do all day but to cater to my needs? I demand that you fix me a meal, and that's the end of the discussion."

She didn't so much as move, and he was pissed off. She had to know that he was having a bad day and should have been nicer to him. Standing up, he went to her and drew back his hand. But the look that she gave him gave him pause.

"You touch me like that, and they'll never find your body." She didn't raise her voice at all, and that terrified him more than her words. "I won't be an abused wife, or so help me, I'll kill you where you stand."

The scary part was that he believed her. She'd kill him right there, and he'd not even know how she'd done it. Backing away from her, he lowered his hand, but he was no less pissed at her. He made his way to the kitchen to find himself something to eat. He'd be afraid for her to fix him something now; she might well poison it. Or spit in it.

He thought about the Troff woman while he was rummaging through the cabinets. He hadn't wanted to send her on the issue, but all the men were out on calls, and he'd been stuck with her. All she'd had to do was arrest one of the Dresden men, Alaric or something like that, and be back in the office in no time. But she'd not done anything she'd been told to do and had supposedly got herself hurt. He no more believed that than he did that she was going to do a good job.

Five women had disappeared in a decade, and he wanted answers. He just knew that the little bastard Dresden was selling them off to other countries and he was making a profit off of it. How else was he one of the richest men in the state? He knew what he was talking about, too. He just needed someone to give him back his job so that he could get him arrested.

"Damned women. They all need to learn their place." He'd been made to hire three women when the laws changed. He didn't understand why it was a part of his department that had to suffer, so he hired them. They only did research on things when he deemed them capable, and to make coffee. The other men in his department were of the same mind as him.

He ended up heating up a can of soup. Thankful for the instructions on the side of the can, he didn't know what he'd have done about a meal. He did think about going out to get something for himself, but he no longer had a car that would pick him up and take him where he wanted to go. Another thing that had been denied him when he'd been forced to retire.

The president had actually made him retire because he'd said that women needed to be knocked around in order to keep them in line. And that children should be beaten in order to keep them out of trouble when they got older. Everyone in his department knew that to be true, and he didn't understand why he thought that was a bad thing.

He'd not hit his wife as yet, but she was pushing him into thinking that she needed to be disciplined. The incident earlier had him believing that he was going to have to take matters into his own hands and show her what was what. Women were stupid as he'd always known, and his wife, he thought, was about as stupid as they came. But she wasn't one to mess with too much. Or he'd have to find himself someplace else to live. He was that frightened of her. But he'd never let on that he was. That's all he needed was for her to think that she'd got the upper hand on him.

He didn't bother cleaning up the mess that he'd made. It wasn't his domain, and he wasn't going to do women's work. It was her fault that he'd made the big mess when he'd spilled the soup on the counter. If she'd just done what he'd told her to do, then she'd have her cleaned kitchen. Not even bothering with putting his bowl in the sink, he made his way to his office.

He tried to bring up his email so that he could see what other changes were going on in his department. But he must have done something wrong, or they'd blocked him out of it because he couldn't get into it no matter what he did. It would be just like the president to have him turned out that way as well, when all he wanted to do was to tell a few people that they'd better be doing their job. He ran a tight ship and didn't want them slacking just because he wasn't there to ride their asses. What did he expect to happen? That they'd just go on like he was there is what he wanted. Now he couldn't even check on things like he should be able to do.

When he couldn't get into anything on his computer at work, he decided to play a couple of games on it. No one would ever know that he wasn't working his tail off. His wife never came into his office unless it was to clean up after him. And she usually did that when he was away at the office. Since he kept a tidy place where he worked, he didn't know what she was going to do with him there all the time. She certainly wouldn't be messing with his schedule.

Just before the news came on, he took himself to the living room. It looked to him like his wife hadn't moved, and he figured that's what she did every other day of the week when he wasn't there to keep an eye on her. As soon as he turned on the television, she put away her puzzles and watched the news with him. They didn't have to talk when the news was on, and he preferred it that way. Even without a job, he wanted things to go on as they had before.

At eight thirty, he was getting ready for bed. He

didn't know if he could sleep all that well; he'd had nothing to do all day that would have worn him out. But he was on a schedule, and he wasn't going to break that simply because his boss had gotten a burr up his ass about something. Besides, he wanted to be ready to go when he was called back to work. There was no way they were going to be able to run his department without him.

Getting up when his alarm went off, he was in the kitchen again waiting for his breakfast. When it didn't seem like she was going to make him anything, he went on a search to find his wife. She was sitting in the living room with her puzzle book in front of her, as if she didn't have anything to do.

"Where's my breakfast?" She told him to make it himself; he didn't have anything to do all day. "I'm going to work today. To see about getting my job back. How can I do that on an empty stomach? Get in the kitchen before I have to slap you around and make it for me."

"I'm not worried about you anymore. You got us into this mess, and I'm not going to be catering to your every whim. I want to have a life too." He told her that her life was making sure that his meals were cooked and the house was cleaned up. "I'm finished with that, too. You told me when we married that I'd be in the lap of luxury. All I've seen from you is you living it up while I stay at home all day waiting for you to come home."

"That's the way it should be. Now get in the kitchen and make me something to eat. I've had enough of you acting out. I will take you to task if you don't do what I tell you." She just kept doing her puzzle, and when he slapped it out of her hand, she simply leaned up and picked it up. His anger was getting the better of him, and when he drew back his fist and hit her, he knew that she was going to retaliate.

When she didn't move, he kicked her with his foot. Telling her to get up and do what he told her did nothing. It wasn't until he noticed all the blood that he thought he might have hurt her badly. Pissed off now that he was going to have to call her an ambulance, he just knew that he was going to be getting into trouble for knocking his wife around. Well, it was no less than she deserved for treating him like she was.

When the ambulance arrived, so did the police. He sat in his chair while the medics worked on his wife. He had to refrain from asking too many questions about her, as he wanted them to think this sort of thing happened all the time. She needed to be made to do her job, and he was just the man to do it.

"Mr. Gravestone, how many times did you hit your wife?" He told the young officer that he'd only hit her the one time, but she'd brought it on herself.

"Did you know that you killed her when you called the ambulance? Your wife suffered from blunt force trauma that shoved her nose up into her brain, killing her where she sat."

"That's not possible. She's just faking it, just like that Troff person. Just make her wake up and get to work. She didn't want to make me breakfast, and I have things to do today." He said he was taking him to jail. "For what? Knocking her around a bit? I told you that she deserved it for not doing as she'd been told. I don't beat her all the time, but she needed to be reminded that I'm not going to be putting up with her bullshit."

"I'm arresting you for the murder of your wife." He was read his rights and kept saying that she was faking it so that she'd not have to work. He'd only hit her the one time, and that shouldn't be enough to kill her. "I'm taking you downtown. Is there anyone that we can call for you? Do you have an attorney?"

"I work for the government. Call my boss. The President. This is all his fault for making me retire. I wouldn't even have this problem but for him. You call him and tell him to come and bail me out." Instead of doing what he'd been told, the officer put him in cuffs and took him out to the cruiser. There was no way that he'd just killed his wife. He'd only hit her the one time, and that couldn't be right. Larry hit on his wife all the time with a ball bat when she needed it, and she never died. "I want to call my boss. The least he can do for me is to bail me out of this. I only hit her the one time, and that's not enough to kill someone."

After five hours, he was finally given his phone so that he could make a call. Peter didn't have an attorney but knew that the president was one. All he had to do was make a couple of calls, and he'd be out of jail so fast that they'd wonder why they even arrested him. He'd done nothing wrong and was pissed off that no one was listening to him. John was finally on the phone with him when he got through.

"Peter, I'm to understand that you killed your wife. Why do you think that I want to have anything to do with you now?" He told him that it was his fault; had he been able to return to work, none of this would have happened. "I don't believe you. Not that it matters. You murdered your wife, and now you're going to have to pay for it. I'm thinking that you're going to get what you deserve."

"I only hit her the one time. People knock around their wives plenty of times, and they never die. I won't believe she's dead until I can see it with my own eyes." He said that someone would have to identify the body, but he couldn't do it. "She's my wife by God, and I'm not going to prison because you decided that I needed to be retired."

John was still laughing when the phone went dead. He didn't know what he was going to do now that he was in jail. There was no one to help him out of this mess, and he didn't like it. There was no way that he'd killed her with a single punch to the face. Someone was going to be kidnapping her soon, and then he'd show them. Damn it, this was all that Troff's fault for being a woman.

Chapter 3

"I just heard about Gravestone. How are you taking it?" Mac told Aaron that she didn't know what to think right now. "Understandable. He keeps claiming that she's been kidnapped and that the president is at fault for his being in jail. He's also blaming you for his being arrested."

"What did I do?" He told her what he'd heard about her just being a woman. "I see. I guess I can understand his way of thinking. He thinks that women are beneath him on such a low level that they shouldn't have the right to vote."

Aaron laughed, and she smiled. "I just wanted to make sure that you heard about it before it hit the papers. I don't know what they're going to say about it, but he really only hit her the one time, and that's all it took." Mac told Aaron that she wasn't surprised by his attitude towards women. He'd been saying the same thing to her since she'd been hired into his department. "He'll be in prison for a long time. John is going to make sure that he's punished to the limit."

"John MacInyre, the president, called you to let you know? You must really be a good friend with him if he went out of his way to notify you." He told her that they were good friends and cats together. "I must say I'm impressed. I had no idea…well, I figured that you knew him, but just not where he'd call you up about something like this."

"He knew that he'd been harassing you, so that's partly it. I think he wanted me to let you know so that you'd know that he's not bothering you anymore. They won't allow him to make calls like the ones he's been doing at the house." She said that would be a relief. "I thought as much. I talked to Zeno, too. We've made up."

He told her what they'd talked about and how it had ended. When he said that they were having dinner with his family tonight, she'd forgotten all about it. Aaron told her that they usually eat at six when the grandparents were coming over because they went to bed at nine.

"I'll have to get ready." She asked about the boot. "I don't have to wear it when they're all around, do I? I mean, they all know that we're mates and that you've healed me."

"No, you'll be fine. We don't have to go anywhere, so no one will see you but us." She said that was wonderful, she hated wearing it in the first place. "It won't be too much longer, and you can stop wearing it altogether Dad said. He thinks another couple of weeks, and you'll be fine to not wear it at all."

She'd broken her ankle when she'd been walking along the sidewalk when Aaron had come out of his office. It was actually the second break, as when she'd fallen the first time, the doctor had told her that it was only a sprain. Falling into Aaron's lap when she'd fallen the second time, she knew that she'd hurt herself worse than before. The pain had been nearly too much for her. Now she was healed because of being mated to Aaron, and she was thrilled. But she had to keep faking it because even though the town knew what they were, tigers, she wasn't going to flaunt that his magic had healed her within days of meeting her.

After getting off the phone with Aaron, she decided to see if she could help with dinner. She knew that when they all got together, LouCinda would do the cooking, and perhaps she could peel some potatoes or something. Anything to stay busy. When she entered the kitchen, she found her crying and rushed to see what had happened.

"It's nothing really. I just get to thinking about my age, and I get sad. I really wanted to have a grandbaby by now, but I can wait a bit longer. No pressure on you, my dear. I have these fits every once in a while. Especially when the boys are coming over. I'm so glad that you're a part of the family now. It's so nice to have someone to talk to." She asked her if she could wait a couple more months. "Are you trying to have a baby now? I didn't know that."

"Yes. Aaron said he'd tell me when I was ovulating and then he'd ask me again. But I want to hold his child so bad, I know just how you feel." They hugged. She couldn't believe how much she loved the older woman and got along with her. "I'm to understand that Frank and Milly, Aaron's grandparents, are coming over tonight as well. You're going to have a full house."

"We're used to it. I never thought to ask you what you thought about them coming over. I'll have to be more careful from now on." Mac asked her why she had to do that. "It's your home, too. I don't want to step on your toes. What if you'd had plans for this evening? I would have messed them up."

"You have the family over anytime you want. I know too that Saturday night is the night that you hold dinners on, so I'd never make plans on that night. It's our house, not just mine and Aaron's. You have to do what you want without thinking that you're going to bother me. We are going to be living together for a long time, and I don't want any tension between us." Getting another hug, she sat down to peel potatoes. "I was going to make baked potatoes, but Zeno asked for mashed, and I can't turn down a request from them. You'll understand when you have your own kids."

"I can't turn down Aaron, so I'm getting a glimpse into what it might be like." The two of them laughed. "I know nothing about babies. Especially not cubs. I think that's what Aaron said they'd be called."

"Yes, that's right. It's not so different than having a regular baby. Except, of course, they do change into kittens when they hit about ten. Some go earlier and some a little later. Aaron changed the first time when he was seven. It scared him badly enough that he didn't shift again until he was eleven. He didn't expect it happen, so he was afraid that he'd done something wrong when he had." She said that Aaron was going to change her after talking to their leap leader. "Yes, he will have to approve it. I don't know why he'd turn him down. Aaron and this whole family has been a part of the leap since he started out being the leader. Aaron could be one if he wanted, and I think that's what the leap lead is going to try to talk him into it one day. But for now, we follow the rules and pay our dues so that there is no trouble from any of us."

"Good." She was about halfway through the potatoes when Milly showed up. Milly and Frank were the boys' grandparents, and they loved Aaron so much that he was spoiled from them. Frank would get himself into trouble once in a while, and Aaron would have to come over to fix whatever he'd done to get it back to working order. But they loved him, so they didn't have too much to get him to fix things around the house.

Just before dinner was ready to be put on the table, the men showed up. They not only set the table for their mom, but they also brought the bowls of food into the dining room. There was going to be plenty to eat, and she was glad for it. The smells alone were enough to have her salivating at the mouth for some of it. By the time they were all seated, she thought that she could eat everything on the table and not feel the least bit bad about it.

They never talked business at the table, she noticed. They did talk loudly and without restraint. It seemed to her that they would argue for the sake of arguing, and it was fun. It was also something that she was going to have to get used to. She loved this family so much that she wondered how she'd made it for so long without them in her life. Especially Aaron.

Clean up was done by the men. Even Franklin and Frank pitched in where they could because she'd been helping cook. They not only put the few leftovers away, but they also loaded the dishwasher and cleaned up the kitchen. It was as pristine as it usually was when there was no one around but the four of them. Mac was so full that she wanted to take a nap.

"Your brother Shawn is in town." That perked her up, and she looked at Aaron to see if he'd known.

"He's staying at the local hotel. I'm running a check on the card he used. Someone by the name of Clair Baker. He said that she'd given it to him to use, looking for his sister and brother. He also had a long visit with Benjamin while he was at the stationhouse, too."

"Did he say what he wanted?" Zeno said that he'd not spoken to him but knew that he'd been upset with his brother. "I can imagine. When Benjamin told me that he was going to be on the straight and narrow, I wondered what Shawn or Dad would have to say about that. He's not bothered me since he apologized to us."

"Is Shawn any meaner than your other brother? Before I forget, your dad will be released soon. I'm to understand that he's been in prison for stealing cars and selling them on the open market. Stupid move if you were to ask me. He was stealing them right off the street in front of his house and selling them to people in the same town." Mac told Alaric that her dad had always been lazy about things and was certainly stupid about everything else. "This will be his third conviction if he causes any trouble around here. We don't take kindly to strangers messing with our town."

"He'll cause trouble when he's in town. He'll think that he owns the place once he sees how small the police department is. He'll try to muscle his way into things that are of no concern to him." Aaron said that he'd try. Mac nodded before continuing. "Something else you should know, he'll have a gun on him. So will Shawn. Shawn hasn't been out of prison long either, but I know for a fact that he's carrying. He also carries a bunch of knives. He thinks that he's good with them. And if I were you, I'd look into his activity concerning that card lady, Baker. I would bet she's more than likely dead someplace and no one knows that she's been robbed, too."

"Thanks. That's a lot of information we might not have gotten without you." She said that she'd been around them longer than they had. "And it shows. I'll have someone in Virginia look into Clair Baker to see what we can find out. If she's dead, then we'll have to look hard into Shawn causing her death."

They talked about her dad and brother until they needed to go home. It hadn't been her plan to take up all the conversation, but she was glad that they were taking her seriously. They were bad people, and when they got here, she was going to have to watch out for them. They'd do worse to her than Benjamin had tried to do when he arrived.

She went up to bed at ten. She was going to sub at the elementary school starting Monday and was excited to have something to do. She'd been lazing about the house for too long, and she needed some activity. Being glad for the exercise equipment in the basement, she knew that she'd be hurting when she was able to walk again without the boot. Usually, she would walk fast when she could, but since she'd been laid up, there was no way that she could do it just yet.

Aaron joined her just as she was getting into the bed. "I wanted to tell you that I'll keep an eye on Roland and Shawn. They'll get the same treatment as your other brother did if they start their shit." She said that she was surprised that Shawn hadn't done anything yet. "So am I, to be honest. But I'll keep an eye on him too. If they think they're going to gang up on you, being that there are two of them, then I'll have one of them arrested. You can't hang out with a known felon when you get out of prison."

"I thought about that. This Baker woman, do you need my help finding things out about her? I can still get into the computers at work and wouldn't mind doing some research on her." He said that would save him a lot of time if she could do that. "I'll start on it first thing in the morning. It'll be nice to have something to occupy my mind other than when I can get out of the house. Your parents have been great about everything, too."

"Mom said she's having so much fun having another woman in the house. She also mentioned us having her a grandbaby. I guess you talked to her today." She told him what she'd walked in on when his mom was in the kitchen. "I knew that she had trouble with depression after Darius was born, but I didn't know she was still fighting with it. That's the reason that we started the Saturday night dinners so that she'd have something to look forward to once a week. And I think we all look forward to it too. I know that I do."

"I love you." He kissed her on the mouth but didn't come any closer. "Something wrong? I thought we could have a little fun tonight since the house is empty again."

"I promised Dad that I'd come back down and keep him company. I think that he and Reagan are going into practice for a while then he'll retire. I don't think that he wants to think about that." She told him to have fun. "Thank you, my dear. I believe that I will. Good night. I love you too."

~*~

Her feet were killing her, and she had three more streets to go. Having a walking mail route was good for her, but right now all she could think about was going home and putting her feet up. But Anna knew that wasn't going to be possible because she had to pick up Harri at preschool, then go home to fix dinner. As soon as she put the last of her mail in the last slot, she was headed back to her car and then the rest of what she had to do today.

"Excuse me." She turned with a smile on her face, thinking that she didn't want to have to deal with anyone today. "You keep delivering my mail to my neighbors. I live at Forty-One Main Street, not Forty."

"I'm just covering this for the person who is on vacation. Have you gone to your post office and talked to them about this?" She said that she'd told the other woman to take care of it. "I'm afraid that my hands are tied. I can't do anything about it. You'll have to go to your local post off—"

"I'm telling you, and you're going to have to fix it. I don't have time to run down to the post office every time my mail goes missing. Just do as you're told, and things will be fixed. Like I said, I'm not going to do it, so you'll have to." She only smiled at the woman, knowing full well that she wasn't going to do anything about it. If her mail was going to the wrong address, then perhaps she'd done that with the company that was mailing it to the wrong address. It was no concern of hers. "Are you listening to me?"

"I am listening to you. Did you get with the company that is mailing it to the wrong address?" Rolling her eyes at her, Anna was ready to give up when the police drove by. Instead of letting them pass, the woman stopped the cruiser by jumping out in front of it. She must have done this before, as the driver had slowed down when he was driving past.

"This woman is stealing my mail by putting it in someone else's mailbox." She tried to explain to the officer that she wasn't doing any such thing, but again, he must have been used to her. He pulled out his notepad and began writing things down. "You'll have to arrest her because she said she's not going to do shit for me until I pay her."

"Lies." The officer said he was taking care of it. "Then do something about the lies that she's spewing. Money was never mentioned. I simply told her that I'm new to this route because of the other woman being on vacation. I never once said that she'd have to pay me in order to get her mail delivered to her."

"Ms. Reynolds, you know that you were told if you caused any more trouble with the mail people, that you were going to have to pick up your mail at the post office. I'm going to ask you how she stole your mail by putting it into someone else's mailbox." She told him that she'd stolen it right out of her box and put it into the neighbor's. "Let me get this straight. You said that she put it in a different mail box? Let me see this mail, and we'll get this straightened out."

"I don't know what I did with it." Nodding, the officer put his notebook away. "Well? Are you going to arrest her? She's stolen my mail and told me that she was going to charge me extra when she had to deliver to my house."

"Did she say that she was going to charge you extra, or did she say that she wanted you to pay extra for her to give you back your mail? It's really important for you to get it right, Ms. Reynolds. There seems to be some kind of misunderstanding about what you were saying." She said she was going to report him. "You do that and make sure you get my name right. It's Alaric Dresden. Just like the town."

When she stomped away, Anna looked at Officer Dresden and told him that she'd done none of those things. He nodded and told her that they'd been having trouble with Ms. Reynolds for some time now. That she gets lonely and causes trouble.

"She scared me a bit. No one told me about her when I took over this route for a couple of weeks." He said that he thought that she was new. "Just temporary. Millicent is off for the next two weeks, then she'll be back. I'll go back to my old route, and she can deal with her."

"They'll make her pick up her mail at the post office now. Which is a good thing. She gets a little high-strung in the summer months when she can track you guys down. We've discovered that she filled out the paperwork wrong for the two companies that send her mail. Usually, Millicent just puts it in her box, and that's the end of it. For a while, anyway. Then she complains about having the mail delivered to the wrong address.

Like I said, she just gets lonely." She asked what she should do about it. "Nothing now. She'll have learned her lesson for a couple of weeks, then she'll go back to her ways. She's harmless."

"Thank you." He told her that it was her pleasure. "I have to go. I have to pick up my little girl from preschool camp. I don't know why it's called that. It's just like every other day at the school." He nodded, and she realized that he more than likely had better things to do than to hang out with a woman who had a four-year-old. "Thanks again."

She was nearly to the mail car when she realized that her feet weren't hurting so badly. Wondering if it had to do with the little break she'd given herself, she decided she was going to do that daily. It wasn't that she wasn't used to walking; she walked ten to twelve miles a day, it was her new shoes that were giving her fits. As soon as she got back to where her car was parked, she got inside and stretched her toes. That felt better, too. On the way to school, she made herself do breathing exercises. There was a reason that she was told to do them, and she'd been putting it off in favor of working so hard.

Anna was widowed before Harri had been born. In fact, she'd not know she was going to have a baby when her husband of five months had died. With the grief that she was dealing with and finding out she was going to have a baby, she had not taken care of herself as well as she should have, and bloomed up to nearly two hundred and twenty-five pounds. On her small frame, she looked sickly. Getting her job back working for the post office, she shed those extra pounds and had trimmed up nicely by walking miles upon miles every day.

Picking up her daughter was a treat that she loved. She was always excited to see her, and Harri would make such a big deal about her being on time, too. She'd never been late to pick her up, but figured that she'd heard one of the others say something, and that was why she was forever praised for her punctuality. After hugs and kisses and a quick word with her teachers, they were on their way.

"I was wondering if we could have pancakes for dinner." Harri usually had something in mind that she wanted to eat when she picked her up. "I want bacon with mine. I had to wash the dishes at school today, and that was Jimmy's fault."

"Why?" She was only about half paying attention as driving was taking all her attention at the moment. "Why is it Jimmy's fault that you had to wash the dishes? I thought that everyone had to help clean up the toys."

"He said a bad word today and had to sit in a time-out. I never say bad words, but because he did,

I had to wash his dishes." She told her that was kind of her. "No, it's not. He said a bad word. Did you not hear me?"

"I heard you. But you doing his dishes because he wasn't able to was nice of you." She mumbled something about the teacher making her do them. "Remember what I told you. We all have to carry our weight when we work together."

"I'm only four years old. I don't know what that means." She didn't talk for a few minutes, and Anna tried not to laugh. "I don't want pancakes now. I want to go to the burger place that has the big toys."

"All right, but then we can't get pizza tomorrow night. We can only eat out once a week. You know the rules." She heard what she would swear was a huff and glanced in the little mirror that showed Harri in the back seat. "It's up to you. But once we get home without eating, then it's going to be pancakes."

"All right. I want pizza tomorrow, so pancakes tonight. Sometimes you're just hard to deal with." She wanted to tell her that she was the same, but kept her mouth shut. There was no point in poking the bear tonight. "How was your walking today, Mommy? Did you get your route done?"

"I did. It has a lot more hills than my normal route, but I got through it." Harri nodded and looked out the window. "How was your day at school—other than having to wash Jimmy's dishes?"

They talked about her papers in her backpack and how she had a note from the teacher. It was about Jimmy saying a bad word so that all the parents would know what had happened. She did wonder what the bad word was, but didn't ask. She might just say it more often if she let her say it now. As soon as they got home, Harri helped her bring in her things, and Anna picked up her own mail. It was nothing but advertisements, and she was all right with that.

After pancakes for supper, it was time for reading. Harri couldn't read as yet, but Anna enjoyed reading to her. They were supposed to read to the children for twenty minutes, but there were times when even half an hour wasn't enough. Harri loved books. Looking through her backpack, she found the note from the teacher and several drawings that Harri had done in class. Her coloring was getting much better all the time.

The note didn't say what the bad word was, but it did make it sound like it had been 'fuck'. He'd been asked to wash the dishes as Harri had pointed out, but thought that he had more important things to do. So he told the teacher to @!#$ off. Anna got a good kick out of that and wondered what his parents would have to say about that, and decided that Harri might not want to hang out with Jimmy anymore.

Getting their clothing ready for the next morning, she bathed her daughter, then took a shower herself. It was nice to be able to do that nowadays, as she didn't worry all that much about Harri getting into things. As she was turning off her light at ten to go to sleep, she thought of Ms. Reynolds and how she was lonely. Anna knew that feeling. She'd been alone for five years now, and it didn't get any better day after day. But she'd not trade her lonely days for time spent with Harri for all the money in the world.

They were running late the next morning. Harri was having a meltdown because she couldn't find her paperwork in her backpack. Then one of her laces broke on her favorite pair of shoes, so she couldn't wear those. Out the door only ten minutes behind, she hurriedly got into the car and sat there for several minutes to calm herself down.

"Mommy, I'm sorry." She told her that it was all right, they got things taken care of. "Will you really buy me laces tonight? Them's my favorite shoes."

"I think that it's about time for you to have a new pair. Those are starting to look bad. But you can keep them." She hoped that she wasn't just setting herself up for another meltdown when she talked about new shoes. "We'll see if we can find some sandals so you will have something to wear this summer. How about that?"

"That sounds good." Letting out a long breath that she'd not realized that she'd been holding, Anna started the car and put it into gear. They might be late to school and work, but they'd be safe while they were doing it. Pulling out into the traffic that was rarely much, they were on their way.

Dropping Harri off at the school, she was on her way a few minutes later. Now she was only a couple of minutes behind as Harri didn't need as much in the way of reassurances as she usually did. Driving to the new post office that she was working from this week and next, she had her things loaded up and ready to go exactly when she needed to leave. Feeling good about herself, she thought that she might well have a better day today simply because she felt like the fates were with her, and that was it.

Until lunch time, she was going at a good clip. It had been a while since she'd had to walk up and down hills, not to mention the number of stairs that were in the new area. Sure that she was going to be ahead all day, she nearly sobbed when Ms. Reynolds was waiting for her at the end of her day.

Chapter 4

Alaric was ready when Ms. Reynolds started after the new delivery person. He'd been hoping for another chance to see the woman and was thrilled when he knew that he was going to have another encounter today. Begging to drive the route he'd done yesterday had got him teased, but he didn't care; she was beautiful, and he wanted to see her again.

"Ms. Reynolds, I have your mail right here. I've not put it in the box yet. You tell me which pieces are giving you trouble, and I'll have a look for them in the future." He took a step back when it looked like the postal worker had things under control. "I know how frustrating it is to get your mail messed up. Even though I work for the service, they still, on occasion, mess mine up as well."

"Let me see what you got there." She handed over the flyers for the new pizza place in town, as well as a couple of pieces of mail he couldn't see. "This is mine. See how it has my name on it, but the wrong address. Are you going to fix it?"

"I am. Right now. I'll slide them into your mailbox or hand them to you. Whichever you prefer."

She put out her hand, and Alaric could see that Ms. Reynolds was a little shocked and put off by the help. "Good. Tomorrow, if you want to meet me right here, I'll hand over your things that go to you, and that'll be the end of it."

"I can't be out here every day, you know. I have things to do in town. You just make sure you get them right." She said that she would for as long as she was on the route. "Good girl. That's all I wanted in the first place." She turned to him. "See? All you have to do is be nice, and that's the way to handle things. We don't need you today. You can go on about your business, officer, and we'll be just fine."

"I'm glad to see that." He stood closer to the postal worker and smiled. "I was wanting to talk to the young lady anyway. I was thinking about asking her out." Ms. Reynolds laughed, and the postal worker stood there. "I didn't introduce myself to you yesterday. My name is Alaric Dresden. You are…?"

"Anna Gibson. I don't date. I have a little girl." He smiled at her and said he didn't mind if they went together. "I mean, I'm not available to date. I'm a widow."

"I didn't think you were married. I didn't see any ring. But I'd really like to take you out to dinner sometime. I'm supposed to be something of a catch to some people around town. You can ask anyone about me." She looked nervous, and he backed away. "I didn't mean anything by it. I just thought you were beautiful and thought it might be fun to have some pizza together. You can even bring your daughter."

"I don't know." She looked around, and he did too. "I don't date. I haven't been on a date since my husband died."

"It's all right. I just thought that I'd ask." He took another step back and continued to smile at her. "No harm done."

"Look, most men don't want to have anything to do with me when they find out that I have a child. It's just the way things work out. Then, when they hear that I'm a widow, they usually turn tail and run in the opposite direction." He said he wasn't like most men. "I can see that." She looked around, and he watched her. She was afraid, but he could also tell that she wanted to go out. "I'm taking Harri to dinner tonight at the pizza place on Maple. It's our once-a-week tradition. If you want to meet us there, that's fine. But I'm not saying that I'm going to sleep with you. I have enough going on in my life without complicating it with sex."

"No sex is fine with me." He handed her one of his business cards and told her that his number was on the back. After giving him her number, she looked cautious again. "I won't harm you or your daughter. I just wanted to get to know you on a personal level and thought that you two might enjoy a night out too. What time should I be there?"

"We go straight from school, so about five. I'm not saying that this is going to be a long-term thing, but I have a feeling that I can trust you for some reason." He thanked her. "No reason for that. I don't trust easily."

"I can see that. I'm glad that you are willing to take a chance with me." He got back in his cruiser and decided that he was going to be on his best behavior. He didn't know why, but he felt a connection with her like he'd never felt with a woman before. Perhaps she was his mate, and he had met someone who was going to finish him. Unlike his brother, he wanted a mate in his life so that he could feel complete.

Going back to the station house, he told Aaron about what had happened with Ms. Reynolds. They both got a kick out of how she was handled, and that made him feel good. He told his brother that he knew she'd be out there every day until Anna left. That made him sort of sad, but if she was his mate, then he was going to go with her. He'd do whatever was necessary to make sure that she was happy. Laughing to himself, he thought about Aaron and how foolish he'd been when he'd been around Mac. And he couldn't wait for things to be just the way that he wanted them.

For the rest of the day, he was finishing up paperwork that he'd been putting off. As soon as it was about time for him to leave, he realized that he'd gotten nothing more done than the basics and was going to blame it on the fact that his mind had been elsewhere. He decided to change, so running home, he was there in no time. When his cell phone rang, he nearly didn't answer the unknown number, but decided that he'd get to it. As soon as he heard her voice, he knew that she was going to cancel on him.

"I want to go home and change so we'll be there a little after five. I didn't think about that when I made the arrangements with you." He said that he'd gone home to change as well and would meet her there. "I still don't know why I'm doing this. I feel like I'm going to be in trouble, and I don't know why."

"I won't hurt you. Not at all if I can help it." She didn't say anything, and he wondered what she was thinking. "How about if I pick you two up and we can go in one car. I'm not sure where you live, but it would be worth the trip to hang out with you two for a bit longer."

"I'd rather take my own car. That way, if things don't work out, I won't have to worry about getting home. I'm not saying that things won't work out for the three of us, but I want you to know that my daughter comes first in all things. She's all I have in the world." He said that he'd never come between them. "See that you don't. I have no trouble at all defending myself if it comes to that."

"Again, I'd never come between the two of you for anything." When he got off the phone, he put her in his contacts so that the next time she called, he'd be able to know it was her. Just as he was about to leave, she called him back. He was laughing when she told him that she was going to have to cancel, as her car wouldn't start. "I can pick you up. I don't mind at all. Besides, you don't want to disappoint your daughter. She seemed to be looking forward to it as much as I am."

"Do you usually play dirty like this?" He might have thought that she was mad, but for the humor in her voice. "All right. I'm at the post office now. I'm going to have to get myself something newer someday, but I don't have the time to look. I have to pick up Harri too. Is that going to be a problem for you?"

"None at all." He could hear the tension in her voice and wondered if it was just him. As soon as he got off the phone with her, he headed to the post office. He didn't know what to think when he saw her car. It looked to be about as old as he was. "I think you're right, you do need to get yourself another car. How old is this one anyway?"

After she told him the year, he thought he'd been right on the money. It was about as old as she was, but she explained that it had been her husband's car and she couldn't part with it. He told her that he understood, and they headed to the school. Harri looked just like a younger version of her mother and seemed to have her attitude, too. She didn't pull any punches when she asked him what he was doing with her mom.

"Her car broke down, and I offered to pick her up. If it's all right with you, I'm going to join you for pizza. I heard that you love it above all other foods." She just gave him the side eye and told him that all kids loved pizza. He nearly laughed but caught himself in time. She told him that he needed to have his own pizza, that her and her mom shared one together. "That's nice. I love mine spicy, so it might be too hot for you."

"You'd be wrong. Are you trying to get into my mom's pants?" He couldn't help it; he burst out laughing, and he could tell that Anna was embarrassed. As soon as she chastised her daughter for what she said, he hoped again that she was his mate. But he was also thinking that she wasn't.

There were no clues to let him think that she was anything but a good friend. It saddened him to no end, but he thought he was right. She wasn't his mate, and he was about as disappointed as he'd ever been about it.

"I'm sorry, Mr. Dresden. Mommy said that I

learn things at school that are better left on the school yard." He told her she was all right, and she looked out the window. As he was pulling out of the school parking lot, his mom called him.

"I need you to come by for a minute. I have some things that need to go to the post office, and I should have done it before now." He said that he was on a date. "I'm sorry, son, but it has to go out tonight. Are you sure that you can't do it for me?"

He looked at his dates tonight and wondered what they'd think about meeting his parents. Instead of speculating on that, he told her what he needed to be doing, and they both seemed to be all right with it. Swinging by his parents' home, he ran in as they said they'd wait in the car to get the package that she had.

"Why didn't you bring her in?" He explained how she had her daughter with her. "You're dating a woman with a child? Good for you. I'd love to meet them. Go and get them."

"Harri, her daughter has her heart set on having pizza tonight." There was a knock at the door, and when the maid answered it, he knew that it was Anna. "Everything all right?"

"Harri needs to use the bathroom. I hope you don't mind. This day is turning out to be something else, isn't it? I mean, I thought it was going to be a good day, but it feels like it's turning to crap." Harri asked where the bathroom was, and Mom took her to it. While she was using the bathroom, he introduced Anna to his family. His mom asked him through their link if she was his mate, and he sadly told her that she wasn't. "I'm sorry about this, Mrs. Dresden. I never thought that we'd be so late getting dinner."

"It's quite all right. We were just going to have dinner ourselves." She said that was nice, and when Harri came back from the bathroom, he kissed his mom and hugged his dad. They were getting a late start, but he was all right with that, too. Going by the post office, laughing a little to wonder if Anna would be delivering it tomorrow, they were on their way to the pizza shop in no time.

Harri did like her pizza hot and spicy. When she ordered her side with double pepperoni, he wanted to pick her up and hug her. Anna ordered black olives for her side, and she seemed to be all right with them ordering a large. She told him that she would take it to work tomorrow and have it while she was walking. While he knew she wasn't his mate, he was still beginning to fall in love with the two of them.

Dinner was a lot better than he thought it would have been, as they both made him laugh a great deal, even at himself. Harri ate a little less than half of her side of the pizza and was beginning to fall asleep in her chair. Picking up the tab, he was happy to pay for all three of them since he'd barged in

After dinner, they went to get some ice cream. He loved ice cream and had been known to eat it just for his dinner. But tonight he was trying to be good and only ordered two scoops instead of the usual four that he normally did. Just as they were ready to leave the ice cream shop, his brother Zeno showed up. He introduced him to the little family and was shocked when he looked so pissed off.

~*~

Zeno thought that he'd been trapped. The woman was his mate, and he couldn't have been more pissed off than if she had put a gun to his head. Not only that, but she had a little girl with her that would be doubly hard to avoid. He looked at his brother and told him that he didn't want him dating her anymore.

"Why not? It's not like you care if she's your mate or not. And I've enjoyed myself with her tonight." He said that he wasn't going to be pushed into something that he didn't want to be. *"You showed up here; I didn't invite you. So get off your high horse and be nice. You're scaring Harri."*

"I'm not kidding you right now, Alaric. I'm not happy with you and the circumstances that you've put me in." He asked how he'd done anything and pointed out again how he'd just shown up on his date. *"You'll not be hanging around her, and that's final. I'm not in the mood*

for you to be fucking with me."

Standing up, he wasn't the least bit surprised to see the anger on his brother's face. He really had barged in on his date, and that was what he'd done. After they left him sitting there with no one to talk to, he decided to head home and try to figure out what to do. He could feel the vein pulsing at his forehead; he was so angry.

He wasn't in a better mood when he got home and decided that he needed something to do, or he was going to explode. After pulling out all the food from his pantry, he started looking at the dates on things. Some of the things had expired years ago, and that pissed him off more that he'd wasted good money on things that he could no longer eat.

Sitting on his couch, Zeno tried to do some breathing exercises so that he could calm his head. It felt like it was going to come up off his head. He was too tense, and that bothered him as well. He had told his family that he didn't want a mate, and now that she was going to be hanging around with Alaric, he'd have to see her every day. Damn it to hell and back, this wasn't fair. He'd made it perfectly clear that he didn't want anything to do with finding a mate, and here they were flaunting her around like she was… well, he didn't know what his brother was doing, but he wasn't going to allow it to happen like this. He didn't want a mate.

He must have dozed off because when he woke, it was nearly ten in the evening. As soon as he got up, he knew that he wasn't going to sleep well when he went to bed, so he decided that he was going to finish what he'd done to the pantry and then try to get some sleep. He had to work tomorrow, and this wasn't helping.

Zeno ended up tossing most of what was in his pantry. He'd started on the fridge too and found that there were things in there that had been worse than his cabinets. He was going to have to make a list of things that he was going to need and go to the grocery store. He didn't have to avoid going now because he knew right where his mate was. Hanging out with his stupid brother.

After making himself a list, it was nearly two in the morning. Going to bed, he was exhausted enough that he didn't have any trouble falling asleep. When his mind went back to his mate, he nearly got up again. But since he had to work, he willed himself to sleep. He knew he was going to have a shitty day tomorrow and was going to blame the woman and her child.

Arriving at work twenty minutes late, his mood was in no better place than it had been last night. Trying his best not to snip at anyone, he was ready to call it a day when Aaron pulled him into his office. He didn't need his big brother busting his chops right now and said that almost as soon as the door was shut.

"Alaric said you were going to be in a mood. I guess she found you last night. I don't know what to say about that, but you'd better be taking it down a notch or two before Earl sets your ass on fire. You know better than to take your mood out on the others." He said that Alaric had set him up. "That's not the way it happened, and you know it."

"All right, he didn't set me up, but why is he dating anyway? It's not like he has time for dates. He should be looking for a house or something, not fucking around with my mate." Aaron asked him if he was listening to what he was saying. "I know what the fuck I'm saying. I don't want a mate, and there he is, thinking that he can date her or something. That's not going to happen."

"What do you care? You said you didn't want her. Why can't he have a little bit of fun with her while you're around?" He growled low, and Aaron laughed. "You just proved my point that I was trying to make earlier when you said you didn't want a mate. That when she comes around, you're going to be in trouble."

"What kind of trouble am I in? None, that I can see. I'm just pissed off at Alaric for flaunting her in my face. Like he has a right to do that." He told him that he has every right to do what he wants, and he was to back off. "What are you going to do if I don't? Nothing. This is between me and Alaric."

"I'm going to tell mom and dad that you found your mate and that you're pissed off about it." That shut him up. He knew that if they knew what he was doing, they'd be very disappointed in him. Zeno didn't even know why he was so angry. Shaking his body to disperse some of his anger, he looked at Aaron. "What?"

"You are loving this, aren't you?" He said that he was actually. "I knew it. You and the rest of you are laughing it up at my expense just because someone came into my life that I want nothing to do with."

"Again, I'm going to ask you why you care so much if Alaric dates her? After the showing of yourself last night, she more than likely won't have anything to do with you anyway. Because of the way you acted around her mom, you made the little girl cry." He flopped down in the chair that was beside the desk in Aaron's office. "You're just lucky that Alaric didn't find you and beat you to shit last night. I had to tell him several times how much it would hurt mom and dad if her two boys were to come to blows over your mate when you've made quite clear you want nothing to do with her."

"I don't." Aaron sat down at his desk and said nothing. "I don't know what's wrong with me, but I don't want Alaric to date her. He's handsy."

He didn't ask why he cared again but kept his mouth shut. After a few minutes of neither of them talking, he made his way out to the desk again to finish what he'd started on yesterday. There seemed to be an endless supply of paperwork that needed to be done, and he just wanted to go home. Though he didn't know what he'd do there. All his cabinets were cleaned out and ready for new things. He was going to the grocery store after work if he made it to the end of the day.

Concentrating on the task in front of him, he finally finished up by the time it was his turn to take the cruiser. His mind had drifted a few times while he was working, to where he was trying to come up with reasons to go and see her. Dumping that idea over getting himself killed, he decided that he'd be better off leaving it alone. He didn't know how that was going to work since he knew nothing about her, but he was going to give it his best shot.

After work, he was in the grocery store when he saw who he thought was the woman. It turned out that it wasn't her, and that pissed him off as well. What did she even do for a living so that he could avoid her? Where was her little girl when she worked? All these hundreds of questions muddled up his mind over and over until he felt his head about to explode again. Putting his things up on the roller, he decided that he was going to go home and go to bed and shut out the world around him. Just as he was paying, a scent hit him in the face, and he knew that it was her.

Turning to glare at her while they were in line, she lifted her chin up and glared right back. He might well have thought that was funny, but he was still pissed that she was around.

"I was here first." She didn't bother saying anything to him, and he was hurting his head was in so much pain. "You'll have to come back when I'm not here. I don't like you hanging around with Alaric either. That's going to stop as well."

"Where the hell do you get off telling me what I'm going to be doing? You don't own me. And I make my own decisions as to whom I'm going to see or not." She put her basket on the roller and looked ready to do battle. "As for you being in here first, I don't give a good damn. I have things to buy, and I'm not going to allow a bully to tell me where I can shop."

"You will not talk to me that way." Her chin, if that was possible, went up a couple of more notches. "I'm your mate, and what I say goes. You'll do as you're told or find yourself out on your ass."

"What do you mean you're my mate? This is the first that I've heard about that." He told her that he could tell by the way she smelled. "So now I smell, do I? You're such a charmer, it's small wonder that every woman in town isn't jumping into your bed. You're an ass hole."

The cashier told him his total, and he was sure that it wasn't the first time. After giving her all the cash he had in his hand, she told him to wait for his change. Grabbing up his bags of food, he was out the door before he could tangle with the bitch from hell again. She was going to have to take it down a few notches, or he was going to set fire to her ass. There was no way that he was going to allow her to talk to him that way and get away with it. He was a tiger by God, and she'd better learn her place.

After getting home, he was carrying his things into his condo when the bag split. Cursing up a storm, he found himself blaming her for that, too. Just as he was cleaning things up, his cell phone rang. Without looking to see who it might be, he barked out his name and said that it had better be important.

"I think it's highly important when I call one of my children." There was a pause just long enough from his mom that he had to reflect on his choices of life at that moment. "What's gotten into you now?"

"Nothing." He knew that wouldn't fly and told her that he'd found his mate and that she was a bitch. "She actually told me that I wasn't going to treat her that way because she was a grown woman."

"What did you say to her? I'm sure that it wasn't

very nice. I'm assuming that it's the girl that Alaric was telling us about." He said he had a big mouth. "Perhaps, but he was just as ticked off as you were when I called him. What did you do to that girl to have her talking to you that way?"

"Why are you assuming that I've done something wrong? What if it had been all on her?" She asked him if it was. "Yes. No. I don't know anymore. I don't want a mate, and Alaric found her for me. He knew better, too. Why is everyone against me right now? I didn't do anything wrong."

"Of course you didn't, yet the entire family is having fun at your expense. Did you know that you made her little girl cry? That's not like you, is it? Not to mention, if she was in the store after you, she must not have known what you were about." He said he didn't put it past her that she was stalking him. "Now you're just being paranoid. Or something anyway. I'm going to ask you again, what is your problem with finding a mate? It's a done deal now. You've found her. What are your plans now that you have?"

"Nothing. I'm going to avoid her. She has a temper, too, did I tell you that? And she took it out on me." She didn't say anything, and that made him think that she was agreeing with him. "Did you also know that I have no idea what she does for a living?"

He thought about how she'd been dressed and

realized that she was a postal worker. As soon as he knew that, he knew something else about her. She was pretty. Not setting well on his already damaged ego, he decided that he was going to stop his mail from coming to his house so that she'd not know anything about him. His mom asked him what he was thinking. He told her.

"Stalking you? I don't think that's how it works. Besides, she'd have to like you some if she decided that stalking you was her best way of getting to know you. I would think, from what you just said, that she'd be avoiding you like you plan to do to her. Sounds like a good solution for both of you. Just avoid each other, and that will make it all right." He asked his mom if she thought that would work. "I don't know Zeno. I'm just saying that you seem to want this not to work, and that's the best way to do it. I don't know that I'd want to have anything to do with you either if you've been spouting off at the mouth like you said you had."

"I can't talk to anyone about this. They all, including you, think that I'm wrong for wanting nothing to do with her, well, I know what I want, and I'm going to prove to you all that my way is going to work. You'll see. She'll be nothing but a faded memory in a few days, and I won't have to have anything to do with her again."

"If you say so." He told his mom that he did

say so and told her that he had to go. Just as he was hanging up the phone, his brother called.

"What the fuck did you do to her? She's been sobbing since I picked her up from the grocery store." Great, another person to be pissed at him. He told Alaric what had happened and his plan. "Yeah, that's a good plan. Stay out of her life." Then he slammed the phone down in his ear, and he wanted to call him back so that he could do the same to him.

Chapter 5

After sending Alaric on his way home, Anna sat in her living room and tried not to cry. What a terrible person Zeno was, and he thought that she was the bad person in all this? Since she'd not known what he was talking about—she did know what mates were, but not on his level of meanness—when he said she was going to listen to him. He'd spouted off other things as well, but none of them made sense to her since she'd met him. She'd been pissed at him since last night when he'd made Harri cry.

"Are you all right, mommy?" She cuddled up next to her daughter and told her that she'd had a bad day. "Was it that old, mean man? I wanted to sock him in the nose, he was so mean to me."

"He's not mad at you, honey." Though in his mind, she didn't know. "He didn't get his way in something, and he's taking it out on the world. We can handle him. We'll just ignore him and go about our day. We won't have to see him anymore after next week anyway. I'm going to go back to my regular route by then, and he'll be nothing to us."

"I don't like him." She didn't either, but held

her daughter. "Can we please go get a burger? We both had a bad day, and we need a treat."

"All right." She didn't feel like cooking anyway, and this would mean that she didn't have any clean up to do either. "You change into your comfy clothes, and we'll hit the burger place in town. You can even have one of those pies they have. We really did have a bad day."

After they got dressed in comfy things to go to town, she hoped her car would start. It was old, she knew that, but it would have to at least wait until her next day off, when she could get to town while Harri was at school and shop for a new car. She had decided that she was nervous about how it decided to just strand her and was worried it would do that again while she was out with Harri.

The drive into town was fun. Harri was making up jokes, what a four-year-old thought of a joke anyway, and telling them to her. Once they ordered their food, her daughter ordered her dessert first thing, so she'd allow her to have it before she changed her mind. They took a seat in the place. It was fairly busy in the restaurant while they were there, and she liked that. Not one that did well with crowds of people, the two of them enjoyed the talk going around the room about the melon festival.

"Since you have no school tomorrow, we'll head

down to the river and see what's going on. I heard from someone that I work with that the tractor pulling is the best thing to watch." Harri ate her meal and wanted more fries. Since she'd already eaten hers, she got her another order and shared them with her. "We do all right together, don't you think, baby girl? I mean, I'm not messing you up too bad, am I?"

"You make me perfect." That was wonderful to hear, and when they were ready to go, dessert eaten too, she headed out to her car and tried to start it. The stupid thing decided that it wasn't going to go, and she was ready to walk home when she thought of Alaric. He'd told her that if she decided to call him, he was going to be in town. Maybe he was still there. "Are we going to get home, mommy? The car won't start."

"I know, baby. I'm going to call Mr. Dresden and see if he's still in town. Maybe we'll have him drop us off at the dealership, and we'll get us a new one. I know what I want." She cheered her on while she was pulling out her cell phone. When he answered, she launched right into what she'd called him for. "I was wondering if you're still in town. My car broke down again. You won't have to take us home if you could just drop me off at the dealership here close to us, and we'll get that car I've been searching for."

"I'm with my brother." She said that it would be all right, she'd call an Uber driver. "No, I can get you. My brother Aaron said we could be late. It won't take but a minute for me to get to you. Where are you anyway?" She told him.

"It's not that far from the car I've been searching for online. I'm sick of depending on a car that's older than I am." He said that she should be able to see him now. "I do see you. You look just like your brothers. I'm sure you've been told that before."

"We all look like our dad. Mom is all right with that. She said that as boys, we'd be too pretty to look like her." She put her phone away when they pulled into the restaurant. "I know nothing about cars, even enough to help you out. This is my brother Aaron. He works with us at the stationhouse."

After shaking his hand, she felt a jolt of something race up her arm. He didn't say anything, and she didn't either. Whatever had happened must have been her imagination, so she let it go. After getting permission to leave her car there for a couple of hours, true to his word, Alaric picked them up and dropped them off at the dealership. The two of them hung around with them to make sure that they were able to go off the lot with a new car rather than being stuck somewhere else.

She knew just what car she wanted and didn't need a salesperson to try to talk her into something else. Aaron was very helpful with Harri, and she wondered why Zeno wasn't more like the rest of his family. Deciding not to think about him anymore today, she smiled at the salesman and told him just what she wanted. If they didn't have it, she would go someplace else.

"We do have that one in stock. However, it's not green but blue. I hope that's all right?" She said it would be so long as he didn't try to pressure her into something more. "No, I wouldn't do that. Besides, Aaron and I go way back, and with him here, I know better than to upsell you."

The paperwork was filled out, and they were going to pick up her old car for her. In a matter of a couple of hours, not only did she have the car that she wanted, but Aaron made sure she got a discount on it, too. Yes, she wondered why Zeno wasn't more like his brothers. They seemed stable.

"I'm sorry about my brother." She said that she would be gone in another week and he'd be on his own. "If you have anymore trouble with him, just let one of us know. There is no point in his treating you the way he has been. Even if you are his mate."

"I didn't pick him out to be anything to me." He said that he knew that. "I just want to get on with my life and avoid him as much as possible. Like I said, just another week on this route and I'll be on my own again. I only picked this up because we traded vacation times. Harri and I are going to go on vacation as soon as school lets out and take the entire two weeks."

"That sounds like fun." She said she was sure that it was going to be and smiled. Aaron grinned back and asked her where they were going. "I'm sure wherever it is you have it planned out to the minute."

"I do, and we'll be going to the happiest place on earth. Don't tell Harri. She'd be bothering me something terrible if she knew where we were going." He promised he wouldn't say a word. "Thank you for going out of your way to help me out. I shouldn't have any more trouble from now on. At least not with the car."

"It was our pleasure, and I'm glad to meet you. You're nothing like I thought you'd be." She asked him if he thought she was some bitch who didn't get her way and took it out on others. When his face turned red, she felt bad. "No, I just thought of you as a woman. I didn't know you'd be so beautiful."

"Now it's my turn to be embarrassed." She laughed a little and told him that she was sorry again. "I didn't mean to embarrass you at all. Just that my mouth gets ahead of my brain and I tend to say things that aren't appropriate."

"My wife says the same thing about herself. She is just as lovely, too. Mac will be jealous that I got to meet you." Thanking him again, she was ready to go when they brought her car around. It was perfect, and she was glad that she'd gotten it tonight. "You drive carefully and don't hesitate to call if you need one of us."

She was ready to get going and got Harri into her car seat. The dealership had brought her old car to their lot, and she was able to get her car seat out of it with the other things that she'd left behind. She knew that Aaron wanted to ask her questions, but she didn't want to have to answer anything right now. One more week to go and she'd be on her own again. She was just glad that she'd been able to get help with her car. It was more than she could have hoped for.

Anna drove the two of them home and was glad that it wasn't too late for her to get Harri in bed. Even though she didn't have school tomorrow, she liked to be on a schedule. As soon as they were home and in front of the television, the two of them started yawning. She'd bet that they'd both sleep in a little late, as stress had a way of doing things like that.

By eight-thirty, they were both in their pajamas and ready for bed. Harri was usually in bed by nine, so this was just a little early for her. Anna went to bed at ten on most nights but wondered if she could make it tonight. It had been a long couple of days for the two of them, and she wanted things to be normal. As soon as her lights were out, she was fighting sleep in order to set her alarm for nine. She usually didn't sleep that late, but she had promised Harri they'd go to the melon fest in the morning, and she was going to keep her promise.

They were both up by seven, and Anna felt good. Harri was in a great mood and didn't put up a fuss when she asked her to wear jeans instead of a dress. She didn't know what kind of activities were going on at the melon fest, but she knew that Harri would want to be a part of it. As soon as they were on their way, she knew today was going to be a better day than they'd had in the last few.

She hated to admit it, but the melon fest was a big disappointment. There were garden tractor pulls, the only thing that the two of them enjoyed, but they were loud and kind of smelly. The arts and crafters were selling things that had to do with melons, all right, but it was more than she wanted to pay for a pair of earrings. Harri got herself a princess halo and had fun running around with it in her hair, but other than that, it was a bust. Trying to think of something else they could do, she heard someone talking about the Conservatory in Columbus, and after looking up reviews, she decided that would be the perfect place to go. As they were walking up the hill to leave the little park, she saw Zeno and his parents.

She tried her best to ignore him, but Harri saw

him before she could tell her. When she started crying, she just knew that people were going to think that she beat her child. She wouldn't even stay on the same sidewalk as Zeno, and she could tell that he was pissed off.

"We're leaving." He asked her what she was doing here, his voice much calmer than she'd ever heard it before, probably due to his parents being there. "We came to see the melon fest and are leaving. You don't have to worry about us being around you anymore."

He nodded and then introduced his father to her. She'd not gotten to meet him the other day when she'd been there. After shaking hands, Harri and her set off for the parking lot so that they could get out of here. She didn't want to have another round with him out in public, especially with his parents so close. She'd had enough of him.

The two of them stopped for another burger and fries and were headed to Columbus. It was Alaric who called her to find out where they were headed, and she didn't mind telling him at all. Once they were at the park, she wanted to go home and cry again. He'd made her so tense in that few-second meeting that she had a pounding headache, as well as her belly was starting to rebel.

Once they started walking around the beautiful

park, she knew that Harri had all but forgotten the man. She was nearly working on it when she saw him again. Talk about stalking, she thought. When she found herself in line to get something to drink for Harri, he said he was sorry. Sorry, wasn't going to cut it, and she told him that.

"Did Alaric tell you where we were going?" He said that they were brothers and he could read his mind. "Well, keep out of my business. Harri and I are here to have some fun after the melon fest, and we don't want you around us. As I said, we're here for a good time."

"I came to tell you how sorry I am. Can I at least do that?" She asked him for what. Invading her privacy or just being a rude bastard? "Everything. I've been rude, and I've invaded your privacy. There's more, too, but I can only say I'm sorry for so much before that's going to be my entire conversation with you."

"I don't think you're funny." He said that he wasn't trying to be that; Alaric was the joker. "He's nice. So is your brother Aaron. I can only think that you should have been beaten more as a child."

"As an adult, too." He stretched his neck and told her he was sorry again. She was paying for Harri's juice when he paid for it. "I got this. It's the least I can do after treating you the way that I did. I had a talk with my grandda, and he isn't happy with me either.

Neither am I. And my grandma won't speak to me until I get you to accept my apology. I am profoundly sorry."

"That's not my fault." He said it wasn't but his own and told her again how sorry he was. "All right. I accept your apology. I'm sorry too for letting you get the better of me. I shouldn't have stooped to your level in your pettiness." He burst out laughing, and she didn't know what she'd said. But he had a nice laugh, and she felt herself smiling.

"You're hard on a man. Thank you." Harri wouldn't look at Zeno, and she didn't blame her. He'd hurt her feelings, and for a four-year-old, that was pretty harsh. "I've been here before. You guys have to go through the butterfly exhibit with me. There are hundreds of butterflies that are flying around, and they land on you."

She could see that Harri wanted to see the butterflies, but she wasn't giving up on her anger toward the man. As they stood in line to enter the exhibit, she could feel her tension building up. While she knew that he was trying to make amends, that didn't mean that she would take his bullshit again. As soon as they entered, she didn't see a single butterfly and wanted to lash out at him again for hurting her daughter. Then one landed on her shoulder.

"Look, Harri." She didn't think about anything

but the fact that Harri allowed Zeno to pick her up so that she could see the butterfly. "He's beautiful, isn't he?"

There were hundreds of them just as he'd said. And the koi fish in the pond were lovely too. They were standing next to the exhibitor when two landed on Harri's hand. She was so delighted that she squealed, scaring away the butterflies.

"Mommy, did you see them?" She said that she did. "They landed right on me like I was a flower. I'm so glad that I wore my pretty coat. They must have thought I was a big flower."

Up until two o'clock, they enjoyed the butterflies. There were other creatures in the dense flowers, but they were also excited about the birds. She did wonder how they got along with the exhibit, but didn't ask. It would be like a feast for the birds to be trapped with so much food.

After two, they decided it was time for some late lunch. They'd eaten on the way in, but now the excitement of the day had made them hungry. There was plenty of different kinds of food to choose from, so they had their meal there. Zeno joined them, but he was standoffish, and she thought that was best for them.

"Mr. Dresden, can you help me with my milk?" She started to say she'd get it, but he opened Harri's carton and handed it back to her. "For a mean man, you did all right."

"I'm sorry for hurting your feelings, too. I have a lot to make up for." Harri set her milk down after taking a sip and looked at him. "I didn't mean to make you cry, and I'm ashamed of myself for doing that."

"You should be. I'm just four, and I have feelings too, you know." He told her that he'd learn not to crush them again. "I should hope so. Your mommy must be really mad at you for making a little girl cry. I liked her."

"I love her very much, and I did disappoint my mom when she found out what a mean person I was." Harri looked at her, then back at Zeno. "Will you forgive me for making you cry? I'll try very hard not to do that again."

"Just remember what my mom says. To think about what you want to say before it goes out of your lips. Don't you, Mommy?" She nodded and wondered when this twenty-something-year-old kid had replaced her daughter. "You are all right now, aren't you?"

"I'm trying to be." Harri finished her meal and wanted to play with the toys that were a part of the cafeteria. Since they were close enough that she could see them, she let her. But reminded her daughter that if she couldn't see her, then she couldn't see her baby girl either.

When she went to play with the toys, other kids joined her. She kept a close eye on her daughter because she didn't know what to think about how people just let their kids roam. Anna wasn't like that. If she were to lose her daughter, then there would be nothing left for her to live for. She looked at Zeno.

"I'd like to talk to you about something. I'm not going to be in Dresden after next week, so you don't have to see us anymore. I won't be in the grocery store or anywhere else in town. I just have to pick up Harri, and that shouldn't be a problem since it wasn't before." He said that he wanted to talk to her as well. "You don't have to say you're sorry anymore. I get it. Your family has beaten you up about how you treated us, and you came to make amends so they'd not be mad at you. Well, I don't want to have anything to do with you either, so we're even on that. We were doing just fine before you came into our lives, and I'm sure we'll do just fine afterwards."

"I want there to be an afterwards." She didn't know what to say to that, so she didn't say anything. "Yes, you're right. My family did beat me up over this thing between us. And my grandma is very disappointed in me. All those things have a lot to do with me trying to say I'm sorry. But the real reason is that I didn't much like myself when I was treating you like shit." He looked frustrated again, and she found herself looking at her daughter. She had a calming effect on her. "Look. Let me start over. I think you might understand what I was saying better if I start where I first started thinking that I didn't want a mate."

"All right. But this doesn't change the fact that I'm going to be out of your life soon." He said he didn't want that. "I think we'd be better off not seeing each other. I'm not seeing anyone, and I like it that way. It's just me and Harri."

"Why is her name Harri?" She asked him what he meant. "Harri? Is it short for Henreitta? Or something like that?"

"No. She's named for her father. Harry Gibson. He killed himself just after we were married. He said it was too much for him to be an adult. He was twenty-two, I was eighteen. We'd been dating for about three years by then, and I thought that he was fine with getting married. He asked me, I didn't force him into anything." He said that he didn't think she had. "His parents believed that I was forcing his hand. I don't know where they came up with that idea. I wanted to wait to get married, but Harry insisted. So just after I graduated from high school, the two of us wed. Three months later, he was dead by his own hand. I had Harri eight months later."

"I'm sorry. That must have been hard." She said that it was, but since she got her daughter things were all right. "Did he leave you a note?"

"Yes. He said that he thought that he could get out of his parents' home and have one of his own. But it was too hard to have a house and a job, too. I never understood his meaning by that. His parents had purchased us the home and everything in it. We hadn't had any bills to speak of, we'd only been married those few months. It wasn't until after I'd had Harri that I realized that he wasn't very mature for a twenty something year old man. And his parents ruled him pretty hard. I think that's why he wanted to get out on his own. To be honest, I don't think it would have lasted between us. I was too young to be the adult in the relationship, and he was too young to be the adult."

Harri came back with one of the toys, and she told her that they had to stay with the others. She wanted to purchase it for herself, and Anna looked at the price tag and then showed it to Harri.

"It's one of those toys they put out so that parents will have to buy it for whiney kids. Are you going to be a whiney kid?" Harri looked torn, but she said that she wasn't going to be whiney. "I'm very proud of you. If you can find something that you can put in your room that will remind you of this day, that would be good. Otherwise, I'm not paying sixty dollars for a stuffed animal." When she went back to the toys, Zeno looked at her.

"I would have bought it just to see the smile on her face." She said she wasn't going to raise a child who thought that whinnying was the only way to get something that otherwise would be off limits. "You're very good at being a parent. I would have brought it all for her and been tapped out at the end of the day."

"She knows that we're on a budget. We don't buy unless it's necessary or a treat. I try very hard not to allow her too many of those, or they're no longer a treat." He said that he understood. "Thank you. You said you wanted to talk to me. About what? I've made it clear that you don't have to worry about us interrupting your life anymore."

"I've thought about having a mate since I was fifteen. And even back then, I knew that she'd be taking over my life. Not in a good way, but just making sure that I'd be right there with her all the time." He watched Harri play with the other kids. "I especially didn't want to have children because I knew that was going to be one more nail in my coffin for being the man that I thought I wanted to be."

"A playboy." He grinned and told her that was it exactly. "I don't see you as a playboy. You seem to have life just where you want it, and it might not necessarily mean you have women around all the time."

"I thought that was the only other option open for me. I was either going to be a playboy, as you said, or a man who was married to one woman and never allowed to see anything else. I had it in my head that I was going to be shackled down with you all the time, and I'd not get to do the things that I wanted to do. Now all I can think about is all the things that I get to see through you and Harri's eyes." She said they weren't going to be mates. "I'd like for us to be. I'd like to start over with you and Harri and become the man that I really and truly am. Not this bastard that made the two of you cry for no other reason than I thought you'd be in the way of me getting things done. I don't know where that thought came from."

"If all you're doing this for is to appease your family, then I'd rather not have anything to do with you. I've had one mama's boy in my life, and I don't need another. He wasn't a good man now that I'm older and can appreciate what we had. He wanted a way out, and I was there for that to happen. I'm not going to be your excuse for you to still be good with your family." He said that he could understand that. He didn't want that either. "Then what do you want? In the event you didn't notice, Harri and I are getting along just fine without you in our lives, and we'll continue to go on without you if you treat us the way you did."

"Are you saying that you'll give me a chance to try and make it up to you?" She said that she didn't know what she was saying right now. "I'll take that. I promise you. You won't have another problem with me so long as you live. And I promise that if we ever have children, I'll never treat Harri like anything but my own child if you'll allow me to."

She thought about what he was saying and didn't say. He was getting pressure from his family, but he also seemed like he wanted to change. So long as he could not hurt Harri, she knew that she could handle him for the next week. After that, it wouldn't matter anymore because she'd be on her own turf and wouldn't have to be around him anymore.

"You have a week to get your act together." He thanked her. "No need for that. If by the end of one week we aren't madly in love, then we'll go our separate ways. Just don't hurt my daughter. Her tears tear me up inside."

"I promise to do everything in my power to make neither one of you cry or be upset with me. And to make you both fall in love with me soon." She thought that was a weird way to say it, but didn't comment. So long as he knew he would get his walking papers if he did anything, then she thought she could give him a chance.

Chapter 6

They had such a wonderful time at the conservatory that he didn't want the day to end. There was a point when Harri started acting out, but Anna pulled her into her arms, and she fell asleep. After about half an hour, she was awake and enjoying herself again. That was when Anna said that they'd have to leave soon because Harri needed to have her dinner.

He didn't mind that he was being shackled down by not just one but two women when he thought about it. And when they ended up getting fried chicken at a chicken place so that Harri could have strips, he enjoyed his dinner alongside Anna and laughed until he thought he might hurt from it. He'd had the most fun all day and wasn't looking forward to going home to his own little condo and missing out on bedtime for the little girl.

"We had fun. And thank you for not buying her everything in the store. That would have been hard to explain to her that she couldn't take it all home." He said he thought that he'd done fairly well in only buying the butterfly stickers. "Yes. I know you wanted to buy her the backpack too, but she wouldn't be able to wear it at school, and that would have been a waste of money for her. She doesn't care that she doesn't need everything so long as you break it down to her level of thinking."

"I'll have to remember that for next time." He was at her house, and he was surprised to know that it was only a rental for her. The for-sale sign out front had her worried, she told him, as she didn't know if the people who bought it would want it as their home or a rental. "I can imagine that would be hard, renting a whole house. I'll have to be more careful in the future for when I buy houses to make sure that the renter will be taken care of when I'm done."

"You have money." It wasn't a question, but he told her that he did. "We have a little saved up, but not enough to buy a house. It's going to be hard for a couple of months to get used to paying a car payment, but we'll be fine after that. I'll just have to pick up some more time at the post office." He started to say that he could help, but caught himself in time.

That he knew would piss her off, and he didn't want to ruin a perfect day with her and Harri by being himself again. Instead, he decided that if she needed anything from him, he'd wait for her to ask. She had a good job and a good head on her shoulders, so he wasn't worried about her having a financial crisis right now. But he would help her if she asked. He really didn't think that she would, though.

After following her home to make sure they got there all right, he headed to his own home. He'd not used his cell phone all day, only to take pictures, and thought that he'd enjoy looking at them later tonight. His mom had messaged him once to ask him how things were going and then later that evening to tell him that she loved him. It was an end to a perfect day, he thought, and he couldn't wait until he got to see Anna and Harri again. He called his mom to tell her what they'd done all day.

"I have some pictures of Harri for you, too." He sent them while he was talking to her. "She's beautiful and so smart. I think she has a better vocabulary than most four-year-olds because her mother talks to her like she's an adult. She's not afraid to bust her on her bottom, too, when she gets a little lippy. I wanted to defend her, but I'm staying out of that for now."

"Good. You don't want to step on her toes since she's been on her own for so long." He said that they work well together. Then he told her about how Harri had gotten her name. "Oh, that poor girl. To have to raise up a child when she was no more a child herself. That's so sad about her husband, too. I wonder if she found him or not. That could be why she distrusts so much."

"I'm the reason that she distrusts me. I blame

that fully on me. But once we talked, I had a wonderful time with her. We went to get dinner together, too. I've never had so much fun." He was grateful that his mom didn't say she told him so, but he could tell himself. Once they were off the phone, he took a shower. He was feeling the effects of the day and wanted to go to bed. He'd been going since before seven this morning, and he was worn out.

After making him a bowl of cereal, he ate it at the counter and rinsed out his bowl. He was going to have to get himself a house soon, even though he had a three-bedroom condo. It would be crowded with the three of them in it, as it only had one bathroom. Still thinking about how big he'd need, he got online and looked homes up. There was plenty to choose from, but he knew nothing as to what Anna and Harri would want in a home.

After an hour of shopping, he headed to bed. It was nearly midnight when he thought of Anna again and smiled. She'd been nice to him all day, and there were a couple of times when he knew she wanted to hit him. But he was learning about having a daughter in his life and a seemingly endless supply of money. He didn't want her spoiled any more than her mother did.

Waking at seven, his usual time to get up, he was at work at eight. He was in such a good mood that he didn't mind running the church crowd and was happy to be there when they started pulling out of the lot. Once a week, they had to control traffic at the local church, and he knew that today the sun was shining in his favor. Getting the traffic flowing in the right direction made him feel good. There hadn't been a fender bender, nor did there seem to be any harsh words over having to stop people from making the streets too overcrowded.

At lunch time, he called Anna. She said it was laundry day and that she and Harri were getting their clothing separated out. He knew how to do laundry, too, and wondered what it would be like to have little things in his wash. He still marveled at how much Harri looked like a shrunk-down version of her mother. Even their shoes matched when they went out.

"I have to change sheets too, so that takes us a bit longer than normal. I usually do them on Saturday, but we were busy all day yesterday, so I'm a day behind." He said that he has a service come in and do his house twice a week, so he didn't have to worry about it. "That must be nice. I've never been able to afford someone to come in and dust, much less clean my house for me. But Harri is neat as a pin, so I don't have much to worry about."

He noticed that she did put her things in her backpack when she had them. So she'd not lose them, she'd told him. When she'd had to explain to him about the character on her pack, she did it in a way that didn't make him feel stupid. She'd told him who she was and how she related to some of the things on the shows that she watched. Harri even had him look up the cartoon so that he'd have a better understanding. He was falling for the kid hard and wondered what it was going to do to his heart if he and her mother couldn't work things out. Suddenly, he was speaking to the little girl.

"I had a lovely time yesterday, and thank you for not making me cry." He told her she was very welcome and that he'd had a good time too. "Most adults hear that mommy has a kid, and they run away. You didn't, so good for you."

Laughing when she handed the phone to her mother, he told her what was said. He could hear Anna telling Harri to watch herself, and that was the end of it. He wondered what it would be like to have an entire family of little Harri's running around and decided that he couldn't do any better than that. She was the perfect little girl for his family, and he wished he'd gotten to know her better the week before. He felt like he'd missed some really good times.

After lunch, he was still feeling good about the day and wondered if they'd allow him to pick them up for dinner tonight. Then he remembered that Harri had school tomorrow and would need to get into bed earlier. He would, too, as he was feeling the effects of not getting a full eight hours of sleep last night. But still, he might go by with a pizza or something just to be able to hang out with them.

"I was wondering what you're doing for dinner tonight. I know that we all have to work, so I was wondering what time I could bring over a pizza." She didn't say anything for a few moments, and he was worried that he'd overstepped his bounds. But she told him that they usually ate at six so that she could be bathed and in bed by nine. "I can do that. Do you want a salad to go with your pizza? I usually have one when I have it. The place where I'm going to pick up has the best house salad dressing."

"That sounds heavenly. We're headed to the grocery store in town now. I have to pick up Lunchables for her lunch for the week." He said that he got off at four today and would be there at six with the pie. "No sodas, however. I don't like her to have them, so I'll pick up some juice too. What do you want to drink? You can have soda, but she can't. I'm brewing tea for the week, too."

"I'll have tea then. That sounds really good." He told her that he didn't drink it sweet when she asked him. "Is that all right? I can drink it if that's what you're making."

"I don't drink it sweet either, and it's decaffeinated. That's the way I can cut down on all the caffeine through the week." He said that sounded good and that he'd see her around six. "We'll be here."

He couldn't bring pizza over every night that he wanted to see her and decided that he'd have to find out what they eat on the weeknight. He could cook, too, but he wasn't going to mess up her kitchen with his skills. He could cook, but he was a messy cook and left behind a wake of pans when he did it. He'd just stick with picking things up for them until he got to know them better.

At four o'clock, he was headed out the door. He'd seen Alaric and Farley, and that made his day. He didn't get to see his younger brother all that often, so he was glad that Farley came by to see him. He taught at the elementary school in Nashport, third grade, and he loved it.

The only time that he was able to see them all once a week was on Saturdays when Mom had them all over. He was going to see what he had to do to make sure that Anna and Harri were a part of the family on Saturdays, too. Sometime.

He was moving in the right direction right now, but knew that he was going to have to slow things down. He also didn't want to pressure her into anything either. He was just going with the flow for now and was having a wonderful time.

Picking up the pizza and salads, he'd even gotten one for Harri, as he knew that she loved salads. If no one wanted it, he'd take it home and use it for work tomorrow. They were delicious, no matter if you ate them the next day or not, and he was all right with having salad two times in the same week. When he showed up at the house, there seemed to be tension in the air, and he didn't know what to do about it.

"She's upset because we're having pizza tonight." He told Anna that he could go and get something else. "No, she'll either eat it or not. I'm not cooking a whole meal for her just because she wanted to decide what we were having for dinner. There is more than her in this house." Anna said that last part like she wanted Harri to hear it, and he wasn't surprised when she came out of her bedroom crying.

"You just don't understand." She said that she didn't and asked Harri to explain herself. "I like to pick dinner on Sunday night. It's my turn."

"What would you have picked?" Harri said she would have picked pizza, but didn't get to. "I don't understand you right now. You're mad because you didn't get to pick pizza as our dinner, and we're having it. He even brought you a salad to have with it. You love salads."

"I do love salads." And just like that, the crisis

was over. "Can I have mine in a bowl? That way I can save some for later if I want it."

"Of course. Now tell Zeno that you're sorry for causing a scene. You didn't have to have a fit when you wanted pizza in the first place." He was told how sorry she was, and he believed her. As soon as they sat down to eat, Harri ate her salad as if she had not eaten for days.

~*~

Shawn couldn't believe that his dad was finally here. Meeting him in the lobby of the hotel, he was glad that he didn't have much in the way of luggage. They would charge him for a double, and he was worried about how much money was on the credit card that he'd stolen. Dad hugged him several times when he saw him.

"I've been thinking about what you said about Benjamin. You said that he wasn't going to be going out on runs with us anymore. I'm thinking that's all right." He asked him why they were family. "Yes, we are, but if he don't want to do it anymore, then we should let him. Besides, it will be nice having someone on the outside to come visit us if we get caught. You have to always think like you're going to get caught, and that makes it better for you. You don't make as many mistakes."

"That's right. I remember you saying that to

me before. I'm never getting caught again. If I do, then I'm going to have death by cops. I'm not going back to prison. It's not the life for me." Dad said that he didn't mind it as he got his three squares a day and a roof over his head. "Yeah, I like that too, but not enough to go back in. I'm finished with the prison system."

"I'm glad to see you, son. Now, tell me what you think is going on with your sister? Mac never was a team player, even when she didn't know any better when she was a kid. I never did cotton to her talking back to me either." He said that Benjamin said she was getting married. "If he's saying that she was getting married, she more than likely is by now. That'll make it harder to get to her money, but not impossible. I heard that she's married to that Dresden family. Now there is some fine money coming from that quarter."

"I don't think I ever found out who she was marrying. How did you find out?" He said that there are a lot of things that he could find out if you knew who to ask. "I suppose so. I've been cooped up in this hotel room just waiting for you to come along. Also, if you're in the room when they come to clean up, they tend to hurry and get out faster. I don't want them finding my shit."

"I don't blame you there. I nearly had me a gun, but my gut told me something was off, and I walked away. I just knew it was going to be someone undercover who was selling it to me." He said that would get him back in prison faster than anything. "Don't I know it. Something else you gotta learn is when to listen to your gut. If it tells you something is off, listen to it. It'll save your life someday."

Dad was forever giving him advice about living on the edge. He'd been heeding his advice for so long that he thought he could write a book on what he had to say. He wouldn't. There was no point in others knowing when to shut up and when to walk away. He thought that was a song, but couldn't remember the name of it right now. If it wasn't a song, it very well should be.

"When do you get to see Mac?" He told his dad that he'd been waiting for him to come to town so that they could work on her together. "Good plan. I don't want this fucked up because we're at cross purposes with each other."

He didn't know what that meant, but he was sure that his dad couldn't explain it. He might have a lot of advice, but he wasn't happy with trying to explain himself when he knew he was right. It was just one of the many things that he had to forget about when dealing with his father. He didn't explain at all, but expected you to do what he wanted when he needed it done.

"We'll call her up and demand that she see us.

Then, while we have her with us, we'll make sure she understands that we come first in her life and that she'd better be paying up. I don't want to have to work for a living, and she's going to be our ticket to that happening. I do have to apply for a job now and again, but that ain't going to mean I'm going to get hired. I'll do what I'm told, but nothing more. Understand?" He didn't, but agreed with his dad. "I also want to see Benjamin. He's going to explain to me why he's suddenly too good to be with us. I don't care if he is or not, but he's not going to just get away with telling me what's going to happen. I'm his father by God, and he's going to tell me where his head is thinking that he's better than us."

"I don't know that he thinks he's better than us, but more like he'd been given a second chance at life." Dad popped him upside his head and told him not to give him any back talk. "Yes, sir." Even for as old as he was, nearly twenty-two next month, he was still afraid of his dad. He could kill you with his bare hands and walk away like nothing had happened.

First thing they did was go and see Benjamin. He wasn't in his cell today as he was in court. He thought that it was Sunday, but realized too late that it was Monday and that the court was in session today. He wondered if his brother would get any time for his part in whatever he'd been doing to get money from their sister, and wanted to know so that he didn't make the same mistakes he'd made. Meeting in the bank was a big no-no. There were too many cameras around to get by with anything, not to mention there was usually a cop or two just hanging around in the event something like this happened. He also forgot to tell his dad something.

"Mac is married, you said. Did she marry the oldest Dresden?" He said that she had. "He's a cop, and Mac is an FBI agent." Dad popped him in the back of the head again.

"That might have been useful to know beforehand, don't you think? Damn it, boy, what have I told you about details? They're as important as getting the job done right. You have to have the right details, or you'll screw up every time. Next time you have that sort of information, it would be good to know sooner rather than it being too late." He thought to himself that he'd given it to him beforehand and was unhappy with the way that his dad was treating him. Like he'd never done anything against the law before. "We'll have to rethink things now. I wish I had known that sooner, but we'll get it taken care of. Is there anything else that I should know before we go and get our asses handed to us? Like, does he carry a gun all the time?"

"He's a cop, so I would guess that he does." This time, he didn't get popped, but his dad was cursing like he'd been told that he was going back to jail. "Mac carries too, I would imagine. She being FBI, and all."

"I wonder how she got that job. Must have not looked into her background too much, or they'd have not given her the clearance. I know that they do a good background check on people before they let them be agents." He didn't know how that worked with the FBI, but he tried his best to stay under the radar when it came to being on their list. He had a buddy once who had been on the most wanted, and he couldn't take a shit without them up his ass about it. "Wouldn't that be funny if we were to get her fired from her job? I think that I'm going to try that and see what I can get going from that. I tell you, son, it would make my day to be able to say that I got my daughter fired from the Feds just because she was related to me."

Dad laughed like it was the funniest thing in the world. He didn't get it, but smiled all the same. There were times when he didn't understand a lot of things going on around him, but keeping his mouth shut had kept him from being made fun of. He'd killed for less than that.

After finding out it was going to be a bust in talking to Benjamin, they made their way to the hotel again. He didn't have a car to drive around, but everything was so close that he didn't mind it so much. Dad, of course, had to complain about having to walk in the heat. He was just glad to be free so that he could walk around when he wanted.

"I've been thinking on Mac. I think we should go and see her today." He said that he didn't know where she lived. "That's easy enough to figure out. We just have to find us the biggest house in town and go from there. Surely with all their money, they'd want to have the biggest of everything. That's the way that I'd do it. Go big or go home is what I always say."

He'd never once heard him say that, but kept his mouth shut. Shawn was beginning to regret having his dad around. Before he'd been there, he'd been able to think what he wanted. Now, if he didn't think like his dad, then he was popped in the back of the head. Like he was some kind of simpleton or something. He was smart enough to get away with murdering people, wasn't he? He'd show him sometime how a real man killed someone.

His dad had been right in finding the biggest house in town and finding his sister. She was there at the house when they got there, and she still wouldn't invite them in. He was sort of all right with that. Big places gave him the willies, and he didn't care for it. As soon as she came out onto the porch with them, he noticed that the big man she was supposed to be married to had come out too. He didn't want any trouble with the big cat.

Benjamin had told him about how he'd marked him up, and that was something else that Mac was going to pay for. He was going to need some surgery to get his hand and chest fixed up, or he'd know the reason why. Frowning to himself, he wondered what that meant, too.

He'd not admit this to anyone, but there were times when something in his head wouldn't make the least bit of sense, and speaking it out loud was even worse. People looked at him cross-eyed. Sometimes the words would get all mixed up in his head, and he'd say them that way too, hoping no one would notice. They noticed all right, and that would piss him off when they'd snicker or make fun of him. Shawn decided that he hated all people and wished they were all dead, leaving him to himself. That included his dad right now, too.

"What is it you want? Before you answer that, I'm not going to give you any money. I'm not going to join your little gang. Nor am I going to look into things for you, like dates that money trucks are going through." He asked if she could really do that, and she glared at him. "Did you hear that Benjamin is going straight? I think it's the greatest thing since you two were put into prison. Why aren't you there now?"

"We got out. And I'll be telling you what you're going to be doing, little girl." Dad looked like he'd gotten a sour piece of candy when he'd said that. Shawn wished he could say things like that off the top of his head. He was better thinking about them when everyone had walked away. "I want you to give us some money. We have things that we're planning, and that requires that you put into this family when I say you will."

"I'm not going to be a part of your family. I thought that I said that." She looked over at the big man, and all he did was nod. "I thought so. So, no gang, nor am I giving you money. Have you ever thought about getting a job? It would save you time in coming up with plans about how to rob someone blind of their money. Also, Shawn, the Feds are looking into the card you have from Baker. Did you kill her?"

"None of your business. You just listen to Dad, and we can be on our way today." He thought that sounded really good and was proud of himself. "For now, you can give us ten grand, and we'll be back later to get more. You got it, and there is no reason why we shouldn't have a piece of it."

"No, and there's every reason why you shouldn't have a part of what I have. I don't like you. Either one of you. And you do remember that I'm a Federal Agent, and so is my husband. If you get nasty with us, we'll call them in to look into your activities. I think you killed Baker, Shawn, and when we find her body, you're going back to prison. This time, there will be no getting out for you either." He asked her why she'd do something like that. "As I said, I don't like either of you coming around. And I won't be blackmailed or whatever it is that you think you're going to do to me. I'm a good deal smarter than both of you combined."

She was at that. When their mom had been alive and around, she would put Mac's paper on the fridge for everyone to see. Even her report card would be hanging there with all 'A's on it. Shawn didn't think she would have gotten dumber as she got older, but smarter, and she always was about as smart as he was stupid. Not that he'd admit that to her.

"Now, if there's nothing else, I'm going to have dinner with Aaron here and go to bed. We're trying to have a baby, and the best time we can have is making one." He thought he was going to throw up in his mouth when he thought of his sister having sex with a shifter. "I don't want you to come back here either. I've had enough of the two of you for several lifetimes."

When the door slammed in their faces after she got up to leave them, Shawn just looked at his Dad and wondered what the hell happened. She'd actually told him no and then went into the house. She'd better be getting her shit in a row, or she was going to be hurting, he thought. Tempted to take out one of his knives and use it on her, he had to figure out a way to get into the house. She sure was lippy, and it was going to cause her some pain.

Chapter 7

Zeno was going to have dinner with his girls tonight, and Anna was cooking. He couldn't wait to try her food, as it was something that she was sharing with him. He'd been invited to her house every night this week, but tonight seemed special. She'd never really cooked for him before. Last night, it had been burgers on the grill and he'd done most of the cooking so tonight was going to be food that she did all on her own.

He had no idea why that made it special, but he was going to enjoy it. For the past several nights, they'd been having a meal together and even Harri was beginning to like him. She'd called him *that man* still, but he was all right with that. As long as she said it in that little girl voice she had, he'd be all right with anything she did. When Anna answered the door, he knew immediately that something had happened.

"They want me to take the Dresden route all the time. Margo isn't coming back from her vacation and now I don't have anyone to work for me on mine. They said they would cover it for me if I were to take the route, but that messes up everything that we talked about. I will be around a lot more." He said he was all right with that. "I'm not. Don't you see? It messes with my picking up Harri after school. She doesn't like it when that changes."

"What time do you usually pick her up? I get off at four every day and can pick her up for you. She can hang out with me until you get off." She shook her head and told him that she usually gets her at four. "Good. I can manage that. I'll just show up to work half an hour earlier and get off that much sooner. It'll be easy for me because the stationhouse is right around the corner from the school."

"What about me being around more? I know that I told you that I'd not be a bother to you, and now you're saying that you'll pick up Harri from school. That sounds the opposite of not bothering you." He laughed and said that he could handle a four-year-old. "I can't handle her on some days, and I'm used to her. You've never spent any time with her on your own."

"We'll have fun. Like I said, it would be easy for me to pick her up and take her to my place. I'm looking for a house for us anyway." She stared at him with an open mouth. "I have the money for it. Just don't worry about it. I'd love your input on the house, but I know we're going through a trial period right now. Aren't we getting along better?"

"Yes, but that's not the point. We'll be around

all the time." He told her he was good with that; he wanted to spend more time with her anyway. "We'll have to talk about rules with her. She knows them, too, but might try and take advantage of you at some point. She's really a good little girl, but she can be a handful at times, too."

"I want to do this. It'll be fun for the two of us to get to know one another. And I think we're moving right along with us getting to know each other enough where she trusts me." She said she'd never have talked to him if she didn't. "I understand that, too. I messed up when I first was around her, and now it's like we're becoming friends. I'd like to get to know you both more, too, if you're all right with that."

"I think we're doing well, too." She looked so frustrated. "I just heard from them about ten minutes ago, so I haven't had time to digest this all. There are certain things that I have to take care of with my old route that I had to. This guy, David, wants my route instead of taking the Dresden one. I don't see how that's fair, but I'm not the one in charge."

They talked about it during the time she was finishing up dinner. Harri was in her room cleaning it up, but he would see her when she'd bring another handful of laundry out to her mom. He'd never been in that part of the house before and was looking forward to what a kid would do about cleaning their room.

He'd always had help when cleaning his room, so didn't have to do it nowadays.

Dinner was on the table about an hour after he showed up. He wasn't worried about it, but helped where he could. There were salads already in the bowls for them, and he teased Harri about him taking her much smaller one for his own. As soon as they sat down at the table, he had to get up to get the wine he'd brought. Harri was having a glass of milk.

They had Million Dollar Chicken. He'd never heard of it before but loved it. She had even cooked him a second helping of the dinner in the event that he liked it. As he was downing his second helping, she told him what kind of things she had to do for her route to be given to this guy named David.

"He just signed onto the post office, so I have to spend a day with him on the route. I hate to do that. No one showed me around on the route that I had. Had I known anything, it would have made dealing with Ms. Reynolds much easier. Now we get along great, but it would have been nice to have had a heads up when I came across her." He told her that Alaric had told him about their first meeting. "Yes, she was trying to get me into trouble with him, but since he was used to her, he told me that she gets lonely at times. She greets me at her mailbox, and we chat for a few minutes before I finish up my route. She's odd but really nice."

"I've had to deal with her a few times. She is odd. But like you said, she can be nice too. I did wonder why we've not had any calls from her about her mail. I just assumed that she was picking it up at the post office now. She has caused a bit of trouble." She told him that she liked her and wanted her to like her. "She does, or we'd have several phone calls about you stealing her mail. I think she does that on purpose so that someone has to deal with her."

After dinner, the three of them cleaned up. Anna loaded the dishwasher, and he and Harri put the things away that were left on the table. It was just like they were a family, the way they worked together. He was looking forward to doing this when they finally got together as a real family. He hoped it was sooner rather than later. He'd already fallen in love with the two of them.

Helping Harri with her homework, reading to her for twenty minutes, he was glad to see that she wanted more. He nearly finished the book when she was called for bathtime, and by the time she was out of the tub, he was ready to leave. He wanted to stay more than anything, but he knew that his trust with the two of them was still being weighted.

He asked when they could talk about the move of his time schedule at work, and she told him it wouldn't start until Wednesday of next week. He was good with that. It would give him plenty of time to cover his shift. Aaron might even help him out with it since he was in so early all the time anyway.

On the way home, he reached out to his brother to tell him what was going on. Just like he had hoped, Aaron was all right with covering his early morning shift and said he'd be all right with him leaving a half an hour early. Earl, their boss was having some tests done this week so he was in charge of the station while he was gone. He wished his brother would take over the job, but he could understand why he wasn't. It was a lot of work, and him just finding his mate. He knew that he didn't want to spend any more time at work than he had to.

"Just make sure when you pick her up, you're okaying it with the teachers first. They might have some kind of rules about strangers picking up kids that don't belong to them." He told him that Anna was taking care that he was on the list to get her. *"I'd see if you can add Mom too. Just in case something happens and you can't make it. That way you won't have to stress about her not getting picked up on time, and I think that Mom would love that."*

"She probably would, but I'll have to talk to Anna about it. Adding Dad, too, might not be such a bad idea but like I said, I need to talk to her. She's very stressful about the changes to Harri's schedule. I don't remember Mom being that stressed out over us." He said because Mom never

messed with changes to their going to school schedule. *"You think? I never remembered it that way."*

"Don't you remember when Dad would have a patient at the clinic and how Mom would keep us in the upstairs? It was because she didn't want things to be off for us when we went to school. She was forever doing that for us. I'm going to be the same way with my kids. Getting stressed out before school can ruin your whole day. Theirs, too, if you're not careful." Zeno said that he didn't remember being stressed out before school, and that was probably why. *"Mom made sure that we went to bed on time, too. It was another thing that I'm going to do.*

"Harri has to have her bath by seven so she can go to bed at nine. She's very good about that, too. Like it's an unwritten rule that they have." He said that they more than likely did. *"I'm glad that I reached out to you. I missed that about Mom keeping us from having to change things up. I'll make sure that I do that when I have her. Anna told me that there would be rules, and I thought she was talking about ice cream before dinner."*

"Don't do that either, or you might find yourself in the dog house again." He promised that he'd not and decided that his brother had a lot of good advice. *"Another thing you might want to do is to make sure you have a car seat for her. I know you know the laws about them, but you don't want to be teased about having her in your car and no car seat."*

He started making notes on things that his brother was telling him, and was very glad that he wasn't making fun of him. He would make sure not only did she have a car seat, but that she was buckled in properly too. There were all kinds of things that he was going to have to do with the little girl. The topmost was to make her safe as she'd be with her mom. Secondly, it was to make sure that nothing ever happened to her while on his time. He'd never forgive himself if something happened to the little girl. She was quickly becoming someone that he loved as much as he already did her mom.

It didn't take him long to get ready for work tomorrow. He was going to start going in early now so that he'd be ready when the time came. He also wanted to make sure that the school had his name and phone number in the event that they couldn't get in touch with Anna. He was going to be her stepdad soon, and he wanted to make sure that the world knew it.

Going to bed tonight, he felt good about the progress he was making in their lives. They sure had made an impact on his life, and he wanted to make sure that they knew it. Tomorrow afternoon, he had an appointment to look at a house. While he knew that Anna couldn't get out of work to go with him, he'd make sure that he took plenty of pictures so that she could see it when he did. He was going to be a girl dad, and he wanted to also have plenty of bathroom space in the house for them. Being sentimental had never felt so good before.

Just before he was ready to close his eyes, Anna called him. He was worried that something had gone wrong, but all she wanted to do was to tell him that she was sorry for overreacting today.

"I had it in my head that things were never going to be right, and I took it out on you." He said he'd never felt like that, and she had been fine. "I talked to Harri, and she said that you picking her up would be all right. But I was to make sure you knew the rules. I have to get you a car seat for her, too. That's something that I don't want to forget having a police officer pick my girl up." They both laughed, and he mentally marked that off of his list to talk to her about.

"We'll do just fine, the two of us. And like I said, we can get to know one another better, too with just the two of us hanging around together." She thought that was going to be the best part. "Thank you for saying that. I already love the little girl and can't wait to see what she grows up to be."

"I don't want to talk about her growing up. She's all I have at the moment, and talking about her growing up will make the time go by faster. I don't need that." Anna sounded teary-eyed and he changed the subject. "Yes, having your parents on the list, too would be a good idea. I'm glad you thought of that." He gave credit to Aaron about that and was glad that he'd been able to bring it up with her. "I need to get off here and get to bed. I hope that I didn't wake you up."

"No. I was just going to bed, but not asleep yet." He wanted to tell her that he'd fallen in love with her, but knew she'd not be ready to hear that. He was trying to be the best he could be for her and was happy when she told him to sleep well. Zeno knew that he would because he'd ended his day talking to her. Yes, he was being sappy again.

~*~

Anna finished up the route in record time today. She wasn't sure how, David had been lagging behind since they started out. He was out of shape, too, for someone that wanted a walking route. She supposed that she'd been as well when she first started out, but she'd been working in it. He didn't seem to understand why they had to stop at each house, even when they didn't have any mail.

"They might have something going out, and you wouldn't know that unless you checked the box. Didn't you learn that when you took the test for a postal career? It was right there in the books." He said that he remembered it, but didn't see any reason for stopping every time. "I just told you. Because they might have mail going out. Or they might need something from you. You just never know what you're going to run into when you're a postal worker."

"I know that this is going to be harder than I thought." She delivered the mail to the next house and waited for him to catch up. He'd been two houses behind her all morning, and she thought that she was never going to be finished with her route. Then he perked up toward the end, and that was why she was able to finish. "Don't you take a break? All the houses have chairs on them that you could just have a seat and rest a bit."

"You're not supposed to do that. They put them there for themselves." He wasn't going to last, she just knew it. And then the postal service would be down another person because he was going to get caught taking a nap on someone's porch when they weren't home. "You really need to follow the rules and do what you're supposed to do. It'll take you a while to get up to speed, but that should be all that's going to keep you from getting done on time. You can't take naps or rest any while you're on the job."

"We'll see about that." Leaving the mail that hadn't been on her route at the post office, she was headed home when her boss asked to speak to her about David. She told her just what she had encountered and what he'd said. She wasn't going to be getting into trouble by him saying that she said he could take a nap, either. She told Dolores just what she thought about him making it too. He wasn't.

"I'll have to keep an eye on him, I'm thinking not just for the first few days either but all the time. If he pulls that shit, he's going to be out of a job and not be hired again either. Does he know how hard it is to get into one of these jobs? It's not easy at all." Anna said that she knew that, and that was why she did everything in her power to make sure she kept the job, too. "I know you do. I hear back from your customers all the time about how you do such a good job."

She had to cover the route one more time with David before she'd be going on her other schedule. It would be great if she could start early and get off in time to pick up Harri, but that was already planned out with her daughter and she was all right with that. Today, she was getting off at four again but since the school knew that she was going to be late today, they'd made arrangements for her to be picked up later. While at the school, she told them about Zeno and his parents picking up Harri.

"We'll put them on the list. Since we know who they are, we won't need a picture identification for them. Mr. Dresden senior has been coming here for years, when there are things like forms that have to go home to the parents. Some of the kids don't have their shots all taken care of, and he goes over the paperwork that we have so that we know which students that need it. Mrs. Dresden has always been helpful at fundraisers too." She said that she'd more than likely always be dropping her off, but on the off chance something happens, they'll be able to do that as well. "Good to know. We'll have everything in place for them when they come to get her. Do they know the safe word for her?"

"Yes, I'll make sure they do. I'd forgotten about that." She would have to tell the whole family the safe word to pick up Harri. If something happened to her and they needed to take her out of school early, then all they'd have to do is tell the teacher *string beans,* and she'd be allow to go with them. She never thought of a reason someone would have to take her out of school early, so she seldom thought about it but she would from now on. "Also, if you could make it so you have their phone numbers too in the event you can't get in touch with me. I don't have them."

"We'll get them if we don't already have them on file. I'm sure that we do, but I'll make sure. I wish other parents were like you in getting things taken care of. We always know when Harri is having someone do something else for her when it's necessary."

"Yes, well, we're all we have but each other and we need to make sure that we're able to communicate well when something goes wrong." Again, she couldn't think of something like that would go wrong but she was sure that for every one thing she could think of there were about fifty more that would pop up. "I'll pick her up tomorrow if everything goes right, and then she'll have Zeno pick her up from then on."

"Yes, we have that." After leaving the school with Harri, Anna went home to try to finish the laundry. She should have finished it yesterday, but Harri had cleaned her room and had found about another load of things that she didn't know if they were clean or not. So she had to wash them to be sure.

Harri had been working on sight words for the past three months. It was going well for the two of them, Anna would quiz her at any time during the time they were together and Harri seemed to know them fairly well. She was glad that she'd gotten her some sight words that she could put around the house on things like chairs and table and other things like that. She could see the word and what it meant easier that way. Anna wanted her daughter to do well when she finally got into first grade. Preschool was going to help her out in that, too.

"I've been thinking that Mr. Dresden isn't going to have the right kind of snacks for me when I go to his house. Can I take some with me so that he knows what to buy?" She told Harri that she'd make sure to give him a list, and since he was doing them a favor by picking her up, she'd pay him to buy the snacks. "That's a good idea, Mommy. You're so smart."

"Thank you. But you keep me on my toes, so I have to be smart. What did you want to wear tomorrow to school? It's art day tomorrow, so it needs to be something that can get stained up." She picked out her shirt and shorts, and Anna cleaned up her shoes. After she went to bed, Anna would lay her clothing out for her so that all she had to do was pull them on and be out the door after breakfast. "Don't forget to tell Zeno thank you for picking you up for us."

"I think he's going to like it." She did too and hoped that her daughter would be good for him. "He said that we wouldn't get into any trouble either. I told him Mommy would spank us both if we got into trouble at his house."

"Yes, I would." After getting dinner on the stove and things set up for tomorrow, Anna set the table for the three of them and didn't even think that Zeno wouldn't be there for dinner. He'd been showing up nightly for the last week and a half, and she didn't even think about it not happening tonight. She wondered if that was a good idea to be used to him showing up all the time. Then she thought that they were trying to get to know one another, and it had to be a good thing. When he showed up at six on the nose, they were ready to sit down to dinner and eat together. She told him about her day when he told her about his. Just like they were a real family.

After dinner, and when they were cleaning up, Harri mentioned snacks for after school. He had an idea what she was talking about, but it wasn't until she got into the pantry to show him what they looked like did he get it. He knew that he was going to have to tell his parents, too in the event that they had her for the afternoon. Taking pictures of the things with his phone, he sent them to his mom and dad, and Mom said she'd get some. He told her not to get a great deal, as they might not have her all that often. Mom called him, and he put it on speaker phone so that Anna and Harri could hear the conversation.

"She could come over for an evening once in a while. She'll need to get to know us as well." He didn't think of that and told his mom that she was brilliant. "Of course I am. I'm your mother after all. We'll just get some of the things that she'll have around, and you'll know that they're here as well. That way, we can be prepared."

"I'm going to be picking her up starting Wednesday, and if she's up for it we'll come by. I'll have to get a car seat that we can all use." Mom said she'd get one too, and that way they'd have it ready for when she came over. "Don't go to too much expense right away. We're still working things out between us.

It's working out, but I'm making sure to take things slowly."

"Mrs. Dresden, I can buy you a car seat for her if you want one. I offered to Zeno, but he said he'd buy one for his car anyway. I don't want to put you out just because I have a little girl that makes things different." Mom told Anna that she was excited to get to know Harri and hoped that she'd spend some time with them. "I'd like that too, but I'm easing her into things like this. Too much will give her a meltdown. You might think that I'm being overly protective, but it's just been the two of us since she was born and neither one of us take well to change. We'll get used to it, but I'm all for easing us both into things. If that's all right with you."

"Of course it is. You do what you need, and we'll follow your lead on things. You're right in easing us all into this. We have to get used to having little ones around us, too. It's been since Darius was born that we've had anyone little in the house." His mom seemed excited for Harri to come over sometimes. "Franklin just had a lovely thought. Why don't you come to the family dinner on Saturday. You're family now, and you should get to know all my boys while you're around. I know that they'll just love Harri and you to pieces."

"If we won't put you out, that would be great."

Mom was excited; he could hear it in her voice when she told her to come over at five on Saturday for dinner. "Can I bring anything to go with the meal? I can bring juices for Harri. She'll eat most anything and will try things that she's never had before. If that doesn't work out, she'll eat a peanut butter sandwich for dinner and be just as happy."

"I'll see what we can do for her. I'm sure that the cook and I can come up with something that she'll eat. And we always have pie for dessert. Tell me she loves pie." Anna said that she loved all kinds of pies and would love that for dessert. "Good. We'll have pie for her if nothing else. She and I will get along just perfectly. I hope so anyway."

After talking to his mom a bit more, he watched Anna read to Harri. He usually did it when he was around, but since he'd been on the phone with his mom, he'd missed the opportunity. He left soon after the story was read, and Harri was put to bed. He could have stayed longer, but he knew that with Anna driving to her old route until the other man was ready to be left on his own, she was having to get up earlier to leave. He wondered how that was going over with her messing with her own schedule.

Going home, he realized that he was bored with just sitting around the house. Since he was going to be looking at houses tomorrow afternoon, he needed to get himself ready for work a little earlier, too. As soon as he put his uniform shirt in the washer, he found some other things that he needed to wash and had a whole load. That was unusual for him, as he rarely did his own laundry when there was someone around to do it. He was spoiled, he realized and decided to start doing things for himself once in a while, so that he could know how to wash things at Anna's home if she needed him to.

After running a dust cloth over his furniture, he was ready to toss his things in the dryer and then ran the vacuum. By the time ten o'clock rolled around, he was about as exhausted as he was when he worked a whole week. No wonder Anna liked to do things in portions over a week's time. He knew that he couldn't clean his whole house in one day again without having a nap at some point. Laughing at himself, he was in bed by the time his clothes were out of the dryer and folded.

Chapter 8

Shawn had a plan. His dad wasn't keen on the plan, but he didn't care. The police were starting to ask questions about his credit card that he'd been using all over town, and he didn't have any answers. They were also telling him that his dad couldn't be hanging out with him, as they were both known criminals and ex-cons. He was going to have to figure out something about that. But first, he was going to get money from his sister.

Mac had been working at the school for the past three days. He knew this because he'd watched her go in and out of the place. He just needed to get her alone sometime so that he could get some money from her, or he wasn't above kidnapping her and having Dresden pay him to get her back. Assuming that he'd want her back. He wasn't sure he'd want her back if he were in that position. Today was the day he was going to get her and then get some money. For all his trouble, he wanted more than just the ten grand that he'd been thinking about getting but he wasn't going to be greedy the first time he got money from her. Ten grand would give him enough money that he'd not have to use the credit card again and get the police off his back.

Since she walked to work every day, he was going to get her on her way to her door. There was no point in his getting her before school. Without her showing up to school, then the police would be involved and that wouldn't give him enough time to get what he wanted. After school, when she was walking home, he'd have a better chance of knocking her around a bit too. That was his plan, and he knew that he had to stick to it. If not, then he'd have to improvise and he'd never been good at that. It would mess him up every time.

He was taking his lucky knife with him so that if she gave him any trouble he'd be able to silence her without fear of being heard. Guns to him were just noisy. He'd use them, but he didn't care for all the sounds that would be made when you had to fire one. His knives had always done him the best good, and he thought that he was an expert at using them. He rarely cut himself anymore when he was slicing someone up.

At three thirty, he was already standing by her car. Of course, she would have driven today when he'd seen her get out of it. She'd not think that he was going to take her, but wanted to talk. As soon as he had her right where he wanted her, he was going to cut her up a bit so that she'd know that he meant business. Then after that, she'd take him in her car where he wanted to go and that would be the end of her. He'd not kill her, but he would show her not to fuck with him anymore. When he wanted money, he was going to get it or she was going to have to pay. It would be a right shame if, after he was done with her, that her husband didn't want her anymore, he thought with a laugh.

"Shawn. What do you want?" She startled him out of his thoughts enough that he couldn't think of what he was supposed to say to her. Pulling out his knife, he told her that she was going to take him to the bank right now. "No, I don't think so. I have things I have to do today, and I don't have time to mess with you. Besides, I told you I wasn't going to give you any money, and I meant that."

"You'll do as I say and do it right now." He reached out to get her, but she slipped by him without him being able to cut her. "I'm not fucking with you now, Mac. You're going to do as you're told, or I'm going to hurt you. I'm thinking you need to be taught a lesson in disobeying me, and I'm going to have fun teaching it to you."

"I don't think so." He'd not counted on her having a gun, and he had to think of something to say to her so that she'd drop it. Having a knife meant that he had to get close to her to slice her, but with a gun she could be far enough away that he'd not be able to touch her before she shot him. "Now you're going to drop the knife, or I'm going to shoot you. I don't care what you want from me, but you just tried to harm me and I'm going to have you arrested. Do as I say, and I won't have to shoot you."

"Come closer to me so that I can get to you. And put that gun away. You know you're not going to shoot me. I'm your baby brother." She pointed out that he was going to hurt her. "Because you have something that I want and you're not handing it over. What's the big deal? You have money, and I don't. Just give me ten grand, and I'll figure out what you're going to be giving me monthly. I might just have to tell your husband what a selfish bitch you are."

"I will shoot you, Shawn. I won't have any trouble just killing you where you stand." He lunged at her, and she didn't move. "I'm not a kid anymore, nor am I afraid of you. You just drop the knife and come along nicely, and I'll have you put in a jail cell next to Dad when he tries the same thing with me."

"This is my plan, not Dad's. And he's pissed off at you, too, for being an FBI agent. Why did you have to go and do something like that? Because you're stupid, that's why. All women are about as dumb as rocks." She asked him about Clair Baker. "She was just a good time that went sour. I told her not to bother me while I was thinking. But she had to, and now look at her. She's dead, and you'll never find her."

"They're looking in the fields around where she lives." That startled him, and he asked her why she'd be doing something like that. "So that's where she is. I'll have to tell the Feds when I take you in. It would be nice to solve one more crime before I have to turn in my badge for retirement." He lunged at her again with the blade of his knife, taking up the distance between the two of them.

He nicked her on her arm, and that's when she fired. He would never believe that she's actually shot him if anyone were to ask, but he was hurting badly in his left leg. When she kicked away his favorite knife, he reached for her again when he felt something hit him in the back. It was the big man, Dresden, and he was hurting him badly.

"She shot me. Right in the leg when I told her not to." He said that he'd cut her. "That was the plan, only I was going to cut her up good so that you'd not want her anymore."

"That's never going to happen. I love her, you moron." He felt the cuffs around his wrist and tried to get away. "I'm going to have to tell you that I have a camera on my vest and that it's been recording you since you lunged at my wife the first time. You should count yourself lucky that I've not killed you yet."

"It's just a bit of money. What's the harm in her paying me so that I can have a bit of it too?" He said that it was the way he was going about it. "By taking her to the bank? You're not making any sense. That's where the money is. And she'd already told me no, so I had to go another route with her."

He was read his rights, like he didn't know them by heart anyway, and taken to jail. His knives were taken back from him, and they even took his best cutter out of his boot before they put him in a cell. He wanted them all back and was afraid that they'd be running some tests on them and catch him with blood in it. He rarely did more than just wipe it down when he was finished with it, so he knew that there was going to be blood in it from all kinds of things he'd been doing.

"I tell you what. You just let me go, and we'll pretend like this didn't happen. I know my rights, and you have to let me go if you have nothing on me. If you were to turn your back on me for just a minute, I can be gone in no time." He was being put in the cruiser that seemed to appear out of nowhere, and was told that it was too late for him. "No, it's not. Just let me go because I'm your brother-in-law. We're related now, and you'd want me to be happy that you'll be hanging around with the family now, don't you?"

"I wouldn't hang around you if we were brothers. So no, I don't care if I get on your good side." He was taken to jail and put into a cell. "The federal judge will be by tomorrow to rule on you threatening and harming a federal officer. Also, you tried to bribe me and I'm also a federal officer. You just can't seem to win now, can you?"

"I'm telling you right now that you're not going to like me being pissed at you. Other people have tried that, and it didn't bode well for them." He said that he wasn't worried about him. "You should be. I'm not a nice person when it comes to people pissing with me. I've been known to leave bodies in my wake."

"Good to know. I'm sure that with that knife we've found on you, as well as the guns that were in your hotel room we'll be able to have a lot of cases solved." He told him he'd not given him permission to be in his room. "You've been using a stolen card from Clair Baker, and we're looking for her body even as we speak. We can use whatever means are necessary to keep you behind bars and in prison."

"I don't want to go back to prison. I have a plan about that too. I'm going to take me out a few cops when I get finished here. And it'll be all your fault." Dresden just walked away, even though he wasn't finished talking to him yet. "Did you hear me? I said that I'm not going back to prison. It's too confining, and they have too many rules. I don't like rules that don't allow me to do what I want. Come back here now so that we can work this out."

The door slammed shut, and he was stuck in the cell. He looked around for his brother, and since he couldn't find him, he figured that he'd either gotten out or was in another part of the jail. It would be just like Benjamin to get himself put in a different cell so that he'd not be able to talk to him. That was another thing that he hated about prison, since he would usually end up in solitary confinement for days on end, he'd have no one that would talk to him. And he enjoyed bouncing ideas off of other people when they were around.

He heard the door open at the other end of the lock-up and heard his dad bitching about being arrested. He didn't know what his dad had done to be in jail, but he hoped they'd put him close to him. His dad would make fun of him for his plan again, but at least he'd have someone to talk to. Shawn didn't like his own company for very long. He'd go stir crazy after a while, and that was something that they didn't want to happen either.

When the door slammed shut again, he heard his dad yelling for him. He was calling out moron, but he knew he was talking to him. He told him that his plan wouldn't work, and now they were both in jail. He asked his dad what they'd caught him doing that he had joined him in jail.

"They came right in and found those guns like

they knew just where they were. Arrested me because I was in there when they were found. That just ain't right." He told him he was sorry. "They found your other knives, too. Just pulled them out from under the mattress like that's where they expected them to be. Never seen a room that had been tossed look so good afterwards. Someone told them what they'd find, and they got you on those, too. You can't have any guns on you when you're an ex-con."

"I know that. Damn it all to fuck and back, I know the rules." His dad told him to watch his mouth, or he'd give him something to curse about. "That has never made sense either. Not to mention you're too far away to make good on your threats. That's like you telling me when I'm crying as a kid, you'd give me something to cry for. I was crying, isn't that enough for you to want to know what was wrong? No, you had to threaten me again. Sometimes I think I get my messed-up words from being around you all the time."

"You take that back." Another thing that he didn't understand, but wasn't going to comment on it. And to think that he wanted someone around so that he could talk to them. He should have stipulated that it wasn't to be his dad. "You keep this up, and I'm going to give them a list of known deaths you caused. That'll get your ass in trouble."

"What about what I know about you, old man?

You should be worrying about what I can tell them about you. I know all your secrets. You'd be better off telling them what you've done because you know that I'm going to make things out bigger than they really are." Dad started cursing, and it made him smile. He didn't know what some of the words were that he was using, but he was sure putting them together nicely. "We'll live a lot longer if we just keep our mouths shut about each other and go on with our lives. I know that I'm not going to lose any sleep over you being in here. At least you can't stab me in the back."

"You think so? Well, you just wait and see." His dad would think on what he was saying and keep his mouth shut. He knew a lot about his dad and wasn't afraid to use it to get out of prison. Not that he was going back. He had a plan for that, too, that would keep him from a life sentence.

~*~

Mac had to have fourteen stitches in her arm, and she was sure that was because Reagan had put them in so small. They were neat as a pin, the stitches, but next week it wouldn't matter at all that she'd been hurt, as Aaron was going to change her into a tiger—they'd finally heard back from the leap leader—and she'd be as good as new.

Since she was going to be changed, they put off trying for a baby. They didn't know what the change would do about the baby, but didn't want to take any chances. They would both be safer with her being a tiger, and she was looking forward to running with Aaron. He and his brothers did it often enough that she thought she'd have a good time with just the two of them. Mac couldn't wait to be able to run with the others, and she was excited about having a baby the next time she ovulated.

Her brother and father were in jail now, and that took a lot of burden off her mind. She'd been waiting on one of them to make a move towards her and was somewhat disappointed that it had gone down so easily. All she'd done was pull her gun, and he sort of crumbled. Although she was glad that Aaron was there, so that he could record the entire thing. She knew that he wanted to shift and take care of Shawn himself, but this would be so much better. No one would come back on him, wondering where the body was.

Then to have her dad in jail, too, was wonderful. He didn't put up much of a fuss either, but he was under lock and key, too, so it was one less thing that they had to worry about. And since Benjamin had been sent to prison too to await trial, she had all her family away from her in less than two days. Someone must have been watching over her since she'd gotten what she'd wanted so quickly.

All they'd wanted from her was money. She

might well have given it to them if they'd been kinder to her. Even as it was, she'd been the only one who had made a success of her life and had money. Of course, being married to Aaron had helped a great deal. He had all the money, and he'd told her that it was all hers if she wanted it. She didn't, but it was nice to be trusted so well with his billions of dollars.

"They've taken the knives to the lab to see what sort of blood they can find on them." She asked Aaron when that was going to happen. "John said that he was going to put a rush on it so that they could get some answers. I told Shawn that there would be a lot of unsolved cases closed, and I wasn't kidding. I think he's been at it for a long time and is just now getting caught. Did you hear him say he wasn't going back to prison? He had a plan that if things got to the point where he was going to be taken down, he was going to make sure that he was killed by cops so that he'd not have to go. I wonder what his plan is now."

"Do you think he has one?" He said that he did, but he didn't know why. Shawn seemed sort of stupid. "He didn't do well in school. I doubt very much he could read if he was questioned about something that he had to read to understand. And he's always had trouble putting together a sentence. Especially if he didn't have time to practice it."

"That explains a lot. Like him telling you to

allow him to cut you. That was in his mind to make happen, and until he got that part done, he couldn't move on in his plan." Mac nodded and told him that she understood that, too. "I'm just glad that the two of them are behind bars. It'll make me sleep better at night just knowing that I don't have to worry about you so much with them out of the picture."

"I'm thrilled. I was always afraid they'd get the jump on me and hurt me before I got the chance to defend myself. I couldn't believe it when I came out of the school, and he was standing by my car. Did he really expect to get away with taking me, or even hurting me for that matter, right out in the view of every teacher in the lot? More than likely, yes. He seemed to have a one-tracked mind, like you said. He just knew that he needed to take me, and since he wanted me, then that was the best way to get me. He really is a moron."

"It's sad, really, that he's gone through his entire adult life and still thinks that just because he wants something, then it should be given to him. Your dad is like that, too, to some extent." She agreed with him. "Was he like that as a kid? I mean, I know you said that your dad was in and out of prison all your life, were the other two as well?"

"Yes. Dad did fifteen years to life for killing our mom. He got out in twenty. We stayed with Grandma until she couldn't take the boys any longer. I was nearly eighteen by then, so I just left home and didn't return. They'd find me every once in a while and knock me around a bit, but I never gave them anything other than what I'd have on me at the time." Aaron said that he wished he'd known her then. "You would have killed them then, where would we be? You'd be in prison, and I'd be pinning away for you." They both laughed, and it felt good to do that after the stress of the day.

"What have you heard from Zeno? Are things going well for him?" He told her that he didn't know that Zeno was playing things close to his vest all the time and wasn't allowing them to get to know them just yet. "I heard that they're having dinner on Saturday with us. I know it must be hard on the little girl. The six of you together are a lot to take on. I'd think that they're doing the right thing about not jumping in with both feet around the family. It would give me nightmares for life if I were just four years old and had to suddenly deal with all of you. Frank said that he was going to bring her something to welcome her to the family. I wonder what he has planned for her."

"He's been out in his wood shop a lot when I go over there. I'm still working on his list of things that he's been fussing with to make himself look busy. The bathroom light scared him the most. It was flickering off and on, and he thought for sure that he was going to set fire to the house. All it had been was a loose connection, and I fixed that right away. He's forever got his tools out for something. I told him I was going to take them from him if he didn't stop doing it. But I find that I can't." She asked what he was doing in the wood shop. "At one time, he made these really beautiful rocking chairs. We all have one around here someplace. We'd have our first Christmas photo taken in them, and then mom would put them up until we were old enough to rock in them. We'll have to find mine so that we can have our child's picture taken in mine."

"What a wonderful tradition to have." She was excited for their child to come along so that she could be a good mom to it. She didn't care if they had a girl or a boy so long as it was healthy. They'd been talking about that since they first made love. How much they wanted children and soon. "I'm going to hire a photographer to take holiday pictures when we have kids. That way, we'll have memories forever. Christmas is still a ways away, but now I'm excited to have it coming around."

They talked about other holidays that were coming up, and they were both happy to be living in the family home. When they'd been looking for a house to buy, Mac had suggested that his parents stay with them when they decided they didn't want to be in charge of the home anymore. All the boys' memories were attached to this house, and she was happy to be able to carry those on with them. Frank and LouCinda were the nicest in-laws she thought that anyone could have. She couldn't wait to make them grandparents again now that Harri was going to be around.

After dinner, they went to the living room and watched some television. There was an interview with Aaron on the news report that talked about getting two criminals off to jail. They didn't mention any names yet as they were waiting on the Feds to take over. For as much crime as they'd committed, and in different states, the Feds wanted to make sure that they stayed behind bars for good. She wanted that too.

Mac thought about her job at the school and decided that she might like to go full-time. Her days were boring to her since Aaron worked all day, and she was enjoying the job a great deal more than she thought that she would. It was the kids mostly, and they were so eager to learn that she found herself eager to teach them. They were going to be the future world leaders someday, and she was going to give them the best education she could while they were in her care.

As they were locking up the house, she thought of Anna. She wanted to be friends with the other woman and wondered how she could do that. Just introducing herself felt like the best move, but if she was honest with herself, she was slightly backward when it came to making friends. She'd have to work harder on that so that the two of them could go shopping together. She did wonder if women did that anymore and decided that she was going to do some research on finding friends. It couldn't hurt, but she knew that she was going to have to make the first move.

"I just heard from Mom. She said that they were going to have steaks on the grill on Saturday night, so that it will be easy to fix. She wants to know if you're all right with that." Mac said that she loved a good steak on the grill. "I think she's hoping that someday you take over the Saturday night dinners so that she can play with the babies she's expecting to have around. She didn't say that, but she hinted at it very hard." She said she'd love to do that, but would like her to do it a bit longer.

"I understand. Mom's been doing it so long that I think she's ready to turn it over to you. You would be good at it. You're so organized. And there's nothing much to do for you. The cook will be able to put together anything you want, so long as they have enough notice on what to have on hand." She pointed out that she'd only been to a handful of them and didn't have a feel for what sort of food they have. "I can help you with that. She'll usually ask one of us what we want, and that's what we have. Like, next week we're having pasta because that's Reagan's favorite thing to have. It doesn't matter to him if it's red or white sauce on it; he just loves everything that has to do with pasta."

"That's a good idea. I thought that she just came up with things off the top of her head. I wouldn't have thought that she catered to her sons still." She laughed. "What would you like for dinner one night? Let me guess. You'd like pork chops with stuffing."

"Nah, I would love to have roasted chickens. I can about eat a whole one all by myself. It's difficult to make for all of us, so I usually get that when I'm there alone with them. You did notice that we had it twice in the last month when my parents were in charge of the kitchen." She said that was why they had chocolate pie too. "Yes, while I don't care for sweets all that much, I can eat just about anything with chocolate in it. I got that from my grandma. She could eat an entire ten-pound box of the things in a week. And not feel the least bit guilty about it."

"She told me that half of loving chocolate was getting to share it with Frank. I guess they pace themselves by having two of the pieces a night until it's all gone. Frank also buys her flowers when he's in trouble. Sometimes, when he's just feeling like she needs them, but she never knows what he's buying them for so is happy that he's gone out of his way to get them for her. I think that your family is about the sweetest people in the world."

"I think that you are just as sweet." He kissed her on the mouth and looked down at her. "How about we practice making a baby tonight, then get up early tomorrow and go to the farmers' market? I've been meaning to take you there since it started. I guess that it's pretty full up this time of year."

She loved it when he'd surprise her with something to do on their Saturdays off. She knew that they'd spend the day together holding hands, too, and commenting on the way things were going for the two of them. And of course, he would make sure that she felt well-loved too. That was the most special part of them being together. It was just being friends, too.

Chapter 9

He'd been picking up Harri for a month now. And other than the one thing, he'd been doing well. There had been no more meltdowns, and he wasn't even going to take the blame for that one. It had been totally on the school, and that's the way he was going to tell people if asked. They shouldn't mess with a four-year-old's schedule like they had.

The school signups for soccer had been set up for Tuesday. That didn't do anything to their schedule as Harri was deemed to be too young to play for the teams. All her grades had been thought to be too young, and it was offered to all the five-year-olds and up. That suited everyone just fine, as it wouldn't be something that they'd have to make special arrangements for.

Then on Tuesday morning, not only did they open it to four-year-olds, but they made the announcement over the loudspeaker to just add to the chaos. Every kid now old enough was supposed to just suddenly have the money for the games, but also have their parents—of which he was not—to sign them up during lunch time at the school. He sort of had a little meltdown himself when Anna called him to tell him what was going on.

It took him several calls and all of his lunch break to go to the school and convince them to allow Harri to play with the other kids, even though he wasn't her relative. He finally had to call his own dad to have him make a few calls to make sure they understood that even though he was only her stepfather, in name only, he was allowed to sign her up and pay the fees. He thought for sure they were going to have him arrested when he started talking to them about ruining a perfectly good day for the kids by announcing it over the loudspeaker that they could now play. Not to mention only giving them that single day to sign up. How were parents supposed to get to the school by lunch, pay the fees, and head back to their jobs in less time than he had for his lunch? But he was Harri and Annas hero for the day, and he couldn't have felt better himself if he'd been on a white horse with a blade in his hand.

Now, here it was about a month later, and he was still riding high on his good deed. Then he found out that Harri was spending the night at his mom's house. Talk about a meltdown, he thought. Anna was about as close to tears as he'd been when Harri had asked him if he was going to be her dad. Kids really could get you in the feels at the worst possible time.

When he picked up Harri after school, he'd

been going to his mom's house. Dad and Mom seemed to enjoy having her over, and it afforded him time to see them interacting together. His mom had such a good time when Harri was over that he wanted to go out and adopt twenty children just so she could spread her love out to all of them. And dad acted like he had invented grandkids; he was having so much fun. The four of them had been doing things around the house, and Mom had allowed Harri to pick out her own room in the house so that when she did come to stay with her, she could have some of her own things around. He thought in the future, not right away, like it was happening.

Not that he thought that his parents wouldn't do a good job with Harri. They had raised them when they'd been four. But she was his little girl, and he didn't want to part with her. It had been okay when he dropped her off at her house with her mom, but to leave her behind with his parents was going to cause him anxiety. She was going to be staying from Friday evening when she got there from school until dinner time on Saturday evening when they all showed up for dinner. Nearly twenty-four whole hours. He had to pause what he was doing so that he could catch his breath. Putting his head between his knees was his next step, and he couldn't believe he was getting this worked up over a stayover at his parents' home.

"What's the matter with you?" He told Anna what was going on, and she tsked at him. "I'm her mother, and I'm not getting as worked up as you are. Something must be wrong with you to be acting like it's the end of the world. I'm not crying right now, and you shouldn't be doing whatever it is that you're doing. You're not helping me."

"I'm sorry. But I've never had to leave her before." She said he should have seen her when she dropped Harri off at preschool the first few times. "I bet you were a mess. I don't know how you've done it this long."

"She's growing up. And as much as I hate to admit it, she's taking this a good deal better than we are." That was true. She'd packed her little overnight case so that he could bring it to her after school. "I checked her bag for her, and the only thing she forgot was slippers. I'm very proud of her right now." Then she burst into tears. "I don't want her to grow up, damn it. She's too little to be wanting to stay someplace overnight."

"Not really." He got glared at. "But really, she's going to be staying with grandma more and more often, so we're going to have to get used to her not being around us all the time. I can barely drop her off at her own house, and you're there. What am I supposed to do when I take her to my mom's and leave her? I'm not cut out to be a father. I want her all for ourselves."

"That's good though, right? It means that we love her a great deal." Anna looked at him with pleading in her eyes, and he agreed with her. "Look at us. We're a mess. And it's only Friday afternoon. You'll pick her up, take her to your mom's, and I'll be there when I get things finished up here. We have to be brave about this because if she thinks that she's upsetting us, she won't stay, and that won't be good for any of us. Especially not your mom. She's looking forward to this as much as Harri is."

"I think my mom will understand." Anna shook her head and said that they weren't going to say a word about how upset they were. "You're right. If Harri thinks that we're not all right with this, she'll never stay with someone again. And while that does have its merits, I don't want to scar her for the rest of her life."

"What if I told you that I had plans for us?" He said they'd have to be good plans. "They are. I want to jump your bones on Friday night. I know that we've been getting close with you staying over and all, but I thought that with Harri gone for the evening, we could have some fun too. We could console one another, too, while we're at it."

"Are you sure? I don't want to pressure you into anything." She promised him that she knew what she was doing. "Yes, I think I can leave her behind if I know that you're going to be mine. But I don't want to rush you into anything."

"It's my idea. So how is that you rushing me? Besides, we've been together for about two months now, and I feel like it's the next step. I want you. However, I want you to know that I've not had sex in over five years, so keep that in mind when you make love to me. There's been no one since Harry." He told her that he was honored that she was ready for him. "I don't know that I'm fully ready for anyone. Like I said, it's been years since I've had sex. But I do want you in my bed and in my life. And the sooner that we get married, for Harri, I think things will go better for her as well. She's asking if you're going to be her daddy, and I don't know what to say to her other than we're working on that. Are we? Working on that, I mean?"

"I have a ring for you." He pulled it out of his pants pocket and handed the box to her. "My Great Aunt on my mother's side left it for me. Well, she left it for the second born to my mom. I think she thought I would be a girl. Anyway, it's beautiful, but if you don't like it, we can get you anything else you'd like." She handed the box back to him, and his heart did a little hiccup.

"You have to do it right." He got down on his knee and took her hand into his. "I don't want a wedding. I had one of those, and I didn't care for all the stress that went with it. Just let us get married at the justice of the peace, and that'll be all that I need. All right?"

"Whatever you wish." He kissed the finger that he was going to put the ring on and pulled the ring out of the box. "I hope this fits. It's not really all that big. But here we go. Anna Gibson, mother of my daughter to be and love of my life, will you make me the happiest man on earth by consenting to marry me? I will take care of you and Harri and any other children that we have for the rest of my days and pamper you in all ways that you need."

"Yes. I will if you would allow me to have your children and not treat my daughter like she's any different than any other children that we might have." He told her that it was easy. "Good. Then yes, I'll marry you."

Since she had the day off, they decided not to change their schedule. She'd gotten someone to trade with her today so that she could get some things done around the house. He'd been taking up most of the weekend, just hanging out with the two of them, and had been in the way of weekend chores.

"By the way, you don't have to worry about your house being sold. I bought it yesterday. I was going to tell you, but I got sidetracked again." She asked him why he'd do that. "I knew it was something that bothered you, and I thought that we seem to have enough room in this house for now, so why not just live here until we find something that we both like. Also, I know we have to take into consideration Harri when buying a house, and so I thought that we could go house hunting with her too. What do you think?"

"I think it's a fantastic idea." She looked at her watch, and he did the same with his phone. "You have to go back to work now. I was hoping that we could talk more. About tonight."

"We'll be fine, and if it doesn't happen, it doesn't. We'll both be fine." She nodded but looked unsure. "You never said how the ring looked? Do you like it or not?"

"I love it. I was just thinking that it will go perfectly with the necklace that I have. It nearly matches the stones in it. I think your great aunt had excellent taste." She showed it off in the bright sunlight. "You'd better get going before I forget the plans for tonight and try to seduce you now. I don't know how good I'll be at it, but it's been a long time for me."

He kissed her goodbye and was out the door before he could change his mind about going to work. He loved Anna very much and wanted to show her how much she meant to him. But like he told her, it would happen or not. It wasn't going to change his love for her at all.

Getting back to work late, he was side-eyed by Earl. He wasn't going to be captain for very much longer, as he had to lose some weight to pass the physical. He was taking it out on all of them, and so far, it had been Aaron who was running interference for them.

Just yesterday, he'd heard that he had to lose two hundred and fifty pounds just to get to a weight they could work with. Then they wanted him to lose at the minimum two hundred more pounds before he could be considered fit for the job. He had weighed in at over six hundred pounds. No wonder he only sat behind the desk anymore. He could barely walk around the place as it was.

It was his turn to go around the town in the cruiser, and for some reason, Earl thought it would be a good idea if two people rode around in it so that they looked good. He didn't care; he got to ride around with his brother, Alaric, and they had a good time. It wasn't often that the two of them would get to work together, and they both said that they missed that.

The day seemed to drag on, and he wished that he'd called off today. He didn't have any reason that would sound good to the captain, but he really wanted out of the office. Just as he was going to pick up Harri, he realized that things were going to be different from now on and that he'd be with the girls in his family all the time. He only hoped that he didn't have another meltdown to go with the one he'd had at lunch with Anna. It wasn't too terribly manly to have to put his head between his knees like a little girl when something wasn't going his way. He knew that he'd be fine; it was just getting out of the house with his dignity that was worrying him. His brothers would never let him live it down if he were to do something like that again.

~*~

Dinner was a hit as usual. LouCinda said that it had all been on Mac as she was going to be taking over the Saturday night meals. Anna thought that it was wonderful that she was handing over the job to someone who would be new to the family. She wondered if she should help out more around their home so that she could take over some of the traditions that had been going on for decades. Anna knew that she'd like that.

She was nervous. And on top of that, she was going to miss her baby girl when she wasn't going home with them. Harri seemed to be having fun at the table with her uncles around. And when she called LouCinda, Grandma, it nearly made everyone at the table weep. They were becoming a family, and it was working out well for all of them. Now she just needed to get through tonight, and she'd feel better about everything. She shouldn't have worried. As soon as they got into the house, he was pressing her against the door and taking her mouth.

They were tearing at one another's clothing even as he made love to her mouth. It was greedy the way he was taking her, and she found that she didn't mind at all. As soon as he pulled her pants down to her thighs, he dropped to the floor and took her pussy into his mouth.

"Yes!" It was all she could manage as she came right away. As soon as he sucked her clit into his mouth, she came twice more before she could get his cock inside of her. Even as they made love right there in the hallway, she knew that she was going to be his forever. "Take me, please. I need to feel your cock inside of me."

"I want that too, but I'm loving the taste of you." She told him that she wanted him again, and he stood up and slammed his cock deep inside of her. Even as she came three more times, she knew on some level that it wasn't enough. There was more, and she wanted it right away.

Even as she was making love with him, Anna worried that she wasn't going to survive him if he continued to make love to her as he was. His cock was filling her in ways that she'd never felt before, and she knew that there was more to come. They made love right against the door, and she couldn't have asked for a better place than where they were doing it right now.

It was epic the way that he was taking her, and she couldn't believe how much she loved this man.

"I love you." He took her mouth even as he pounded her pussy. As soon as he stiffened, she braced herself for his climax. It was better than she hoped it would be, and she nearly passed out when he cried out that he was coming. She must have blacked out at some point because she found herself in her bed with Zeno beside her. Rolling to be atop of him, she sat across his body so that his cock was right where she needed it to be. She sat up a bit, and he helped her slide his cock inside of her. She rode him gently, enjoying the feel of him deep inside of her.

"How are you feeling?" She told him that she'd never been better. "I was hoping you'd say that. You feel good right where you are right now." She grinned.

"I could do this all day and never tire of you being inside of me." She nearly lost her rhythm when he surged his hips upward, taking her to new heights. "You're very good at keeping me on my toes. I love the feeling of you deep inside of me."

"I love being there too." When he took her shirt off, not even realizing that she was still partially dressed, he sat up enough that he could take her breast into his mouth. "You taste like the best sex I've ever had."

They both laughed, and she knew that she was

going to be happy to be with Zeno for the rest of her life. When she leaned down and kissed him, he rolled her to her back and still made love to her slowly. As he touched her skin, she could swear that he was touching her entire body. Even as he made love to her, she touched him as well. There was something so wonderful about being able to touch him where she wanted and how she wanted.

"I love you, Anna. With all that I am. I hate that we started out on the wrong footing, and that's all my fault. I hope someday I can make it—" She put her hand over his mouth.

"It's all finished now. We are a couple, and that's all that matters." He nodded and kissed her hand, still over his mouth. "Make me come again, then I'm going to sleep. I've had a good day and now all I can think about is having you beside me for the rest of our days together."

"My pleasure." He did make love to her, but slowly as before. He touched her breasts and had her nipples become painfully hard. As he pulled one up to where he could pull it into his mouth, she wrapped her legs around his hips and rode him slowly.

They made love throughout the night. Even when she came, she wanted more from him. And she knew that he was going to make love to her every night like this, and her heart soared. He was all she needed in the world, and she couldn't believe how lucky she'd been in having him find her when he did.

Waking up once to go to the bathroom, she was scared when she found she wasn't alone in the bed. It took her several minutes to realize that it was Zeno and that he was all right to be there. After coming back to bed, she was pulled into his arms again and fell to sleep. She'd only remembered that she didn't have to work tomorrow at the last minute and was glad that she'd not set her alarm. Anna had a feeling that she was going to sleep late for the first time in her adult life.

When she woke, she was alone in the bed. She could hear the shower going and wondered how long Zeno had been up. Getting up, she was sore just enough to know that some of the muscles that she'd used last night weren't ones that she normally used. Getting into the shower with Zeno, she was happy that he was glad to see her.

"I'll wash your hair for you if you scrub my back." She nearly fell when he massaged her head for her in a way that made her so relaxed. "You can't go to sleep right now. I have plans for us for the rest of the day. The realtor called me, and she has three houses that she wants us to look at."

"All right." She thought about Harri and wondered if she was being good. She said as much to

Zeno. "I don't want to make a bad impression on your parents by the way I raised her. She and I were all we had, and I've never left her with anyone before."

"But me. And I love that you trusted me with her." She scrubbed his back, and he made love to her against the shower stall. "I can't seem to get enough of you."

"Nor I you. This is fantastic, the way that we make love to each other. It's like we've known each other for all our lives." He said that he felt the same way. "I hope that Harri is all right with you living here. You will be, won't you? I mean, there is no point in us skirting around living together now, is there?"

"No. And I'd love to live here with you and Harri. We'll be one little family." She laughed and reached for a towel when he turned the water off. "I have to go into work for a couple of hours tomorrow, and then I thought that the three of us would look at more houses. I think it's great that we're involving Harri in the process."

"She'll no doubt have an opinion on all of them." It made her laugh to think about her daughter being in the process of house buying. She would have an opinion, and she thought that was funny. "All she's ever talked about is having her own yard. With a swing set. I guess your parents are going to be putting up one at their house for the grandkids."

"I'd heard about that. The kids will love going to stay with them, I think. I hope that my mom is having a good time. I guess they were going to go shopping for things for her bedroom at the main house." She said that she'd heard that and nearly screamed when she was dressed in something she'd been thinking about. "I should have warned you about that. You'll be able to change your clothing into whatever you want with just a thought. I love it for when I'm running behind, but I didn't think to tell you about it. It's nice, I think."

"It just startled me." She changed her clothing twice more before she found something that she could wear in the warmer weather. "This could come in handy when I'm running late in the morning, too. I can change into my uniform with just thinking about it and not have to worry about ironing it. I love this perk with being with you."

"I see. You're just out for my magic." She was embarrassed, but when he laughed, she joined him. "There will be more, I'm sure, but since Mac came into the family, I won't know what to tell you what it will be. It'll be different for all the women that come into the family, I'm thinking."

They headed to the first house on the list and were disappointed in it. There were enough bedrooms, but it needed to be updated on all the things in the house. Especially the kitchen, which looked like it was decades old and needed to be stripped down to the studs and start over. They didn't want that sort of project for themselves, just starting out.

The second house wasn't much better. While the kitchen had been updated in the last decade, the rest of the house had been neglected. The carpets were worn in places and frayed. The fireplace didn't work as it was supposed to be gas. Then there were the bathrooms. They didn't look like they'd ever been updated since the house was built in the late sixties.

The third house had promise, but they were asking way too much for it. Even Zeno thought so, and he had lots of money. It would need some work on it, but again, the price was too high for a fixer-upper. As soon as they were finished for the day, they made their way home to take a nap. She really needed one after getting so very little sleep last night.

She'd not heard from Harri in all the time she was with her grandma. It worried her a little that she might not be having a good time, but she knew that Harri could roll with things that most kids her age wouldn't. She supposed that it would tell if she wanted to stay again. Anna knew that she'd be better handling it now that she'd done it once, but didn't want to make a habit of it. She missed her daughter something terrible and wanted to have her close at all times.

Not that it was possible. She really was growing

up and would be five soon. As soon as practice began for soccer, she'd be around different kids than she went to school with, and that would be good. The more social she was, the better she would be in her friendships. Anna couldn't count on one hand how many friends she had that she could go and have lunch with, and was looking forward to having fun with the women of the family. Mac had already told her that they'd have lunch once a week from now on just to catch up. Her life was pretty boring, so she didn't know what they'd have to talk about.

After taking a nap, she felt better. It had been a long night, and she didn't mind at all not getting any sleep. She was no longer as sore as she'd been earlier but was exhausted in a good sort of way. Eating some lunch with Zeno was fun too, and they both sat in the living room to watch television until it was time to go to pick up Harri after dinner.

"I heard from my mom. She wanted me to thank you for allowing Harri to spend the night. I guess they've been shopping all day and are going out to lunch." She asked why she didn't call her. "She doesn't have a connection with you yet. You'll have to make a connection with all of my family so that they can talk to you when they need you. I never thought about that until Mom mentioned it."

He had to explain how that had to happen,

and she was slightly nervous about them biting her. But she'd do it so that she could have the connection that they all used. Zeno even showed her how it worked with his connection to her, and she thought that was fantastic. To be able to reach out to him when she thought of something, especially when she was working, would be good. She wasn't supposed to have her phone on her while working, and this would make it so that no one would know that they were talking. There was a lot to the mating business that she loved, and she knew that there was going to be a great deal more for her to understand, too.

They were at the dinner early enough that she got to get hugs from Harri. She got a little bit anxious when they hugged, but since Harri was all right with it, so was she. There was going to be more outings with grandma, and she knew that was something that she was going to have to get used to.

Chapter 10

Reagan was seeing his last patient of the day when he realized that he was supposed to have dinner with his parents tonight. Sometimes they would call one of them up and have them over for dinner. Tonight was his turn, and he thought that he was looking forward to it, but now he wasn't. It had been a long day, and he wasn't up to making small talk tonight. He would have called to cancel, but he knew that they would be disappointed that he couldn't make it, and that would hurt his heart. He loved his parents very much and never wanted them to be disappointed in him.

"Mrs. Runion, how are you feeling today?" She told him of her aches and pains, and he, laughing, told her that for her age, she should expect a few of those. She would be ninety-three on her next birthday. She made him wish that all his patients were like her in getting around. But she drank bourbon once a day and swore that was what was keeping her young. "Let me get with your chart here and see what this visit is about."

"I have a cold. I've had one before, but I can't seem to shake this one. Do you suppose it's pneumonia?

It wouldn't surprise me to no end that I'd get this late in my life. That sort of stuff kills you if you're not careful." He listened to her lungs and found them to be fairly clear. "That's good to know. I've been worrying over some details of my going home stuff and didn't want to do that until I have all my ducks in a row. You'd better have yours all set up, too. You just never know when you're going to go and see your maker."

"I know, and I do. I have everything going to my parents in the event that I die before they do." He thought this was a morbid conversation and decided to change the subject. "How are you resting? Sleeping any better since the last time I saw you? I know you said you weren't getting enough rest and had to nap during the day. I need a nap sometimes too and highly recommend them to everyone." She laughed, and he smiled with her. She would laugh like a braying jackass when something tickled her, and he enjoyed that about her, too. When she laughed like she did, you knew that she was enjoying a good story or a joke.

"I got me a place all planned out where I nap. It's right there on my sunporch with the sun coming in on me. There's a nice fan too that I have blowing on me. Might be where I got this cold, but I'm not too worried about it. You'll fix me right up." He said he'd do his best, and she patted him on the cheek. "You're a good boy, Reagan. I ain't never had me a doctor like you before. You take good care of me, and you never make me feel like I'm wasting your time either. As I said, you're a good boy. Your parents did right by you, and you should tell them that all the time."

"I tell them I love them at least twice a day when I see them. I'm having dinner with them tonight, as a matter of fact." She asked him why he was wasting time on her when he could be with his mom and pop. "They know that I have to work. And I think following in my dad's footsteps has made him proud of me more."

"Well, of course you did. There ain't nothing better than a doctor in the family either. I'm betting right now he's as proud of you as he is of that new granddaughter of his. She's a mighty cute little thing. Knows her manners too." He said that he loved her too. "I'm betting you all do. She'll bring more love into that family than you ever thought possible. Children do that. Not mine, but I don't want to talk about them today. Pissed me off something terrible. They want to put me in a nursing home, so I'm not all by myself all the time. That's another reason that I've lived so long, I'm not having to deal with them anymore. Kids can be a wonderful thing, but they can also be a pain in the backside." He laughed with her again.

After giving her a prescription for some cold medicine, he saw her out. His dad would be happy to know that she was still getting around so good. He thought that she had been one of his first patients when he started out his practice. He'd been taking more and more of his dad's patients over the last few months. Dad and Mom wanted to travel now that they were all out of the house, and he couldn't wait for them to get going.

Closing up the clinic, he drove himself home. After a quick change, he was on his way to his parents' house, feeling better about the visit all the time. He knew, too, that Mac and Aaron would be around and thought that he'd enjoy seeing them as well. He loved his family and loved to be around them as much as he could.

Dinner was good, as usual. They had pork chops on the grill, his favorite thing to have with mashed potatoes and gravy. For dessert, there were pies. Since he knew that he'd be taking some home with him, he only ate one slice of pie from each of the three offered and had a good laugh with his mom. She didn't bake well, so she left that up to the cook, but today she had supervised, she told him.

After telling his dad about Mrs. Runion, they sat around the living room and talked about how old she was when she first came to him as a patient. It was hard to believe that she'd been anything but old to him, but Dad told him that at one time she had been the belle of the ball to some people.

"Her family isn't much to talk about. They've never given her much of her due when it came to her health. But now that they want to put her into a nursing home, she might have to knock a few heads around. Like her husband before her, she wants to die at home and not have to have the fuss of the hospital. I believe she's going to do what she wants and damn her kids." Mom said that she used to come in with her kids and keep them in line with just a look. Dad agreed with a laugh. "She would only have to give them a look, and they knew that they were going to get it when they got home. I'm betting that she never once hesitated to give them a swat to the bottom when they needed it, no matter if they were in public or not."

"She puts me on notice sometimes, too, when I'm seeing her. If she doesn't agree with whatever I've told her, I know she's going to do as she wants when she gets home." Dad told him that was more than likely right. "I'm going to miss her when she goes. I don't think it's going to be for a while yet, but I will miss her."

"I will too. Even now, when I see her around town, I wonder what her secret to living so long is. She gets around better than most fifty-year-olds I know." Reagan agreed with his dad, bringing up a couple of patients who were just like he said. "They get old before their time, and it shows on them. I think people realize that they're in their sixties and just give up. I'm just getting to the good part of my life right now and wouldn't have it any other way. Your mom and I are going to go see the world once I've given you the last of my people, and there will be no turning back the clock for us. We're going to live each day like it's our last."

"Like grandma and grandpa." They were good examples of people not giving up because they hit a mark in their lives that had them giving up. "Sometimes I find myself a little sore because I moved something that I should have had help with, and I think of grandda. He's still out there working on things like he's got all the time in the world. Sometimes, like me, he should ask for help, but Aaron is around to get him out of fixes."

"He does at that. Aaron spends more time out there refixing things that dad had gotten into his head would work better than he does just visiting them." Dad laughed. "I swear to you, he didn't tinker with things like he does now. I think he does it to get Aaron out there to help him out. Aaron thinks so, too. But they get along in their little plays, and that's all that matters."

They spoke about how Harri had spent the night with them and how much fun they had. Grandda had made little Harri a rocking chair so that she'd have one, and he said he was making more of them before his time was up. None of them wanted to talk about that, but they all appreciated that he was thinking ahead.

"She sure did like that gift. She told me that she didn't have any grandparents who wanted to have anything to do with her. I hadn't realized until I spoke to Anna that her husband had killed himself before she was born. And that his parents blamed it on her. I don't know why, but I assumed that he'd been there for the two of them after the little one had been born." Reagan said that according to Zeno, she'd not even known she was pregnant when he died. "I didn't know that either. Poor little family. I'm so glad that they're a part of ours now. Do you suppose they'll ever want to have anything to do with that little girl? I can't imagine doing that if one of you boys died. I'd want to be a part of her life even more so."

He didn't want to talk about dying anymore and said as much. His mom said he was right; there had to be better topics than death to talk about. Dad said that he wanted them to know that they'd had everything taken care of in the event something happened to them, then he changed the subject to the fall season.

"I'm going to get me some of those blow-up things for the yard. I'm betting that little Harri will enjoy then." Mom said she'd been looking at all kinds of things they could do for Harri, and their plans were endless. "She sure can tell you what she's about when she has something to say. I love that about her. She talks really well for a four-year-old, too, if you ask me."

"That has to do with the way that Anna speaks to her. She talks to her like she's just another adult that she has to deal with, and that's what made her vocabulary so strong. I can't wait to see her out on the soccer field this fall. She'll be bossing the kids around to do a good job that I think they'll do well." They all three laughed about the little girl. She was what grandda called a pistol, and he really was looking forward to the other brothers having wives and then babies. He said as much to his parents.

"What about you, son? You looking forward to having a mate? I'm betting there is one out there for all of you." He said that he didn't have time to look. "Maybe she'll fall in your lap like Mac did to your brother. That was the best story that I'd ever heard."

Mac had been power walking when she'd come around the stationhouse. Her ankle had been hurt before coming to town, and it was bothering her that day. Aaron had just come out of the office, and she literally fell into his lap, breaking her ankle again. She'd been told it was just a sprain from before, but they all knew that it was something more.

After nine o'clock, he was ready to go home. Dad didn't want him to leave and asked him if he wanted to stay. He said that he couldn't as he had to work in the morning for half a day and didn't want to be late. And he would be if he stayed at his parents' house. It was too tempting to sleep late in his old room, and he'd never hear the end of it from his patients.

Getting home so late, he almost didn't see the box until it was too late. As it was, he tripped over it as he was going into the condo. Putting it on the table, he was glad that it finally came as it was for the office. He had things delivered to his home on the off chance the office was closed when something came around. He would take it into work in the morning and have it put away before his first patient arrived. He'd just have to make sure that he got up in time to leave early. Just as he was going to bed, Zeno reached out to him.

"It's going to be fine. I keep telling myself that." He grinned and asked him what had happened. *"Harri fell down the stairs and is complaining about a headache. I don't want to take her to the hospital until I have to, but you tell me what to do."*

"Take her in, and I'll be in soon." He got up and dressed in clean clothes so he'd be able to see the little girl. *"If her head hurts, it might be nothing, but there is no point in taking any chances. I'll order some tests to be run, and then we'll see from there. I wouldn't worry too much if she's not throwing up. She's not, is she?"*

"No, but she does have quite a knot on the back of

her head." He told him to put ice on it, and he'd see her soon. *"Thank you, Reagan. I didn't want to freak out, but Anna said to give you a call. That's the reason that I went a little overboard and reached out to you. If she's worried, I am as well."*

Even as he was driving into the hospital, he was calling in orders for her. He'd been told that the department wasn't all that busy and would take her right back. As he'd told his brother, it was more than likely nothing at all, but there was no point in guessing when there was a perfectly good hospital right in town. Just as he arrived, they were taking her for an MRI of her head to be sure.

~*~

Zeno was better when he saw his brother. He was really trying his best not to freak out, but Anna was worried, so he was too. He knew in the back of his mind this might happen someday when she'd be hurt; he never expected it to be so soon after he moved into the house.

"I was going to ban her from using the stairs again, but I knew that wouldn't work." Reagan laughed and told him that he had to buck up; things like this happened all the time. "Believe it or not, you're not helping me right now. I wanted a peaceful night at home, and she comes tumbling down the stairs like she didn't have any legs. I couldn't breathe for the first five minutes."

"We'll get the tests back soon, and you'll see, everything is all right. Now, if she has a concussion, I might keep her overnight. I don't want her to be sick at home when we can take care of her right here. If I were you, I'd call Mom and Dad to let them know. They'll be worried too, but at least they won't find out about it from someone else." He said he'd call them now. "Call them. If you reach out to them, they're going to feel your panic and be twice as worried."

"Won't they hear it in my voice?" Reagan told him that he could be better when he spoke to him. "All right, I'll call them. I'm not sure what they can do until you get the results back. But I'm betting they come down here, too."

"You can bet they will just to be sure. It's going to be like that for all the kids, I'm betting." Zeno decided that he was going to remain calm and call his parents. If they asked if they should come down here, he was going to tell them no; they had it under control. He didn't, but would say that so that they'd not worry. He was going to be a basket case if all his kids ended up in the emergency department while they were growing up. He didn't remember having to spend much time in here, but he'd been a tiger shifter and could heal himself.

Not only did she have a concussion, but she also needed to have six stitches where she'd hit her head.

He was never so happy to know that his brother was taking care of Harri as he would have been if it had been his dad. She was in good hands.

He didn't even mind that Harri was a bit whiny. He would have been sobbing his shirt off had it happened to him, and he told her so. She said that she wanted to sleep, and they'd allow her to, but only for a short period of time. She'd have to be monitored so that she didn't get worse, and he was fine with her being in the hospital. Anna seemed to be taking it better than he was, and he envied her. The next time would be easier, she told him, and that didn't really help his state of mind at all.

Harri got sick in the middle of the night twice, and they took her to have another MRI. She also got an X-ray. When there was no change in the images, they decided that it was stress. Harri was doing much better after they got her bed changed and gave her something for her belly. After that, with the exception of her being woke up on occasion, she slept through the night and into breakfast the next morning. He found himself worried about that, too, but it was Anna who assured him that she was going to be fine.

"She fell when she was just learning to walk. She hit the corner of the coffee table that we no longer have and busted her head wide open. She had to have twenty-three stitches then, and she had to stay in the hospital for three days while they decided that I was a good enough mother to take her home. I was just as anxious as they were about my ability to take care of her after that. I was a new mom on my own, and I was sure they were going to take her from me." He asked what she did after that. "I got smarter around the furniture that we had in the rooms. I took out the coffee table and a few other items so she'd not fall. And I was extra careful when she was moving around, too. I've had to take her once more to the emergency department, and that was just a little while back. She'd gotten hurt on the playground at school, and the school nurse said she was fine. I didn't believe her, which turned out to be a good thing as she'd broken her arm. I will never trust a school nurse again with my child."

"Good to know. So you're an old hand at her getting hurt. I kind of freaked out a bit. I probably didn't help you in dealing with the situation." She said she'd been ready to leave him at home while she came into have her seen. "Don't do that. I would really freak out if you did that to me. I promise I'll do better in the future, and you won't have to leave me at home."

They decided to keep her for another day, and he relayed the message to his parents. They didn't come in like he thought they would, but came in the next afternoon. Of course, they had gifts for their grandbaby and had to step out of the room when they were shown her stitches. As soon as she was able to keep clear broth down, they decided that she was on the mend and released her sooner. It was nearly four o'clock when they finally got her home and into bed. She was still hurting, but not nearly as bad as she'd been at the hospital. He vowed to pamper her until she complained at home while she was recuperating.

Dad had some advice when they got her home. "Don't do too much with her. Just let her rest. And if she can tolerate it, give her some ice cream rather than food. It'll be good on her belly, and she'll enjoy getting away with something that she normally wouldn't be allowed to do." He told him he'd buy some on the way home. "Not ice cream but popsicles. That way it won't settle in her belly wrong."

"I'll get her all the popsicles she can eat." Dad hugged him and then thanked him for calling them. "It was Reagan who mentioned it. I was going to call you when we heard anything, but he said it would be better if we called then. I love you, Dad."

"And I love you, son." After another quick hug from his mom, they were headed out of the hospital. After stopping at the store, he was armed with any kind of treat that she'd want. Putting her to bed after they got home, he sat in the living room and had himself a little meltdown, too. Her first boo-boo with him around, and he thought he'd done all right for himself.

"What are you going to do when she starts dating?" He said that was easy, she wasn't going to be dating at all. "What are you going to do, become your big bad tiger when the boys start coming around? That'll go over well. You'll have her so angry with you that you won't be able to be around her for her being pissed off."

"That's better than her dating. Besides, you don't know what men like me would do to a little girl like she's always going to be to me. If I have to sit outside her door as my tiger, I'm going to do it just to keep her safe. I failed today, but I won't again. She'll have all her parts just where they're supposed to be so long as I'm around." She told him that he was being goofy. "Maybe I am, but I want her to know that I'm going to protect her at all costs."

"Well, I hope we have a houseful of little girls just so you can protect them. I wish I had had someone in my life who would have protected me. But then I might not have had Harri, and she's worth any price I had to pay for being married so young. I'd do it all again." He kissed her on the mouth. "Not that I really care, but what was that for? You're going to be happy with a houseful of girls?"

"So long as you carry them and they're healthy, I don't care what we have. They could all be human for all I care." She said she'd not thought of them being cats. "There's a chance that they could all be something different, but like I said, I don't care."

"I love you so much, Zeno." He told her that he loved her as well. "I am looking forward to the next fifty years with you or so."

"Same here. We'll have a good life, and our kids will be perfect. Even if they're not, we'll love them to pieces." He thought of the next few years and hoped they'd have more children soon. But it was up to her and her body. That's the way it should be.

Harri woke up once in the middle of the night. She wasn't sick but hungry. Giving her a choice of treats, she decided on a grape one that he loved as well. When she went back to sleep after eating it, he was happy to watch her sleep. Whispering to her, he kissed her on the forehead.

"You scared me a little bit. I'm all right now, but let's not run down the stairs again." She told him, "Okay," and he had to smile. "I love you, Harri. You're the best part of your mom."

"I want to have a little brother or sister soon. Can you talk to mom about getting one for me?" He promised her that he would as soon as she was all healed up. "Good. I want a puppy, too, but I don't think that's going to work with you being a cat, huh?"

"I never thought about that. We had a puppy when I was a kid that sort of grew up to love us all."

She told him that she wanted to see his kitty soon, and he was all right with that. The sooner she got used to him being around, the less afraid she'd be if he had to save her from something someday. "You rest now, and I'll talk to you in the morning. I love you."

"And I love you, Dad." When she rolled over and went to sleep, he sat there for twenty minutes just thinking about what she'd said to him. He'd treasure this night forever because she'd called him dad. Going to be with Anna, he decided that he didn't care if they moved into a bigger house; he knew that they'd have to soon if the kids started coming, but for now, he was as happy as he could be living in the little house with his tiny little family.

Harri was still complaining the next day, but since she was able to eat her treats then, she seemed to be all right. After she laid on the couch all day, he decided that they needed to get something for dinner rather than have Anna cook again. She would do it, he knew, but there was no reason for it when things were still going on with Harri.

She would have school the next morning, and after getting with Reagan to find out if she should go or not, he left it up to them. If she was feeling better, there was no reason for her to stay home. But he did write her a note saying that she wasn't to go out at recess nor have gym for the next week. There was no point in her having another headache when there was no reason for it. Harri seemed to be all right with the idea of her going to school, too.

"I miss my friends." He said that was why he went to work so that he could be around other people. "Do all police officers hang out together all the time, Daddy?"

"Not usually, but some do. In a small town like this one, it stands to reason that we've become close. I think that's true for all small town stationhouses. There are just a few of us, and we seem to get along fairly well." She called him daddy again, and he couldn't help but feel proud of that. "You will probably be in the same group of classmates until you graduate from high school. They'll be lasting friends too. Ones that you've grown up with."

"I'd like that." She was watching television when he got up to go into the kitchen. Anna was in there looking in the cabinets. He told her his plan for dinner, and she smiled at him.

"You're ruining us for cooking at home. But I can't help but be all right with it. It's better than having to come up with something to eat and then cook it. I'm all for not having to cook tonight. What were you thinking?" He told her that he could have just about anything delivered. "Then we'll figure it out later. For now, I want to pamper my kid and hope she doesn't get hurt again for a while."

He was all for that. He'd been terrified when she'd fallen down the stairs and had hit her head. He wondered how other parents did it and decided that he didn't want to know. He had his own little pity party this morning, and he never wanted to feel like that again. Helplessness wasn't something that he did well with.

Before You Go...

HELP AN AUTHOR

write a review

THANK YOU!

Share your voice and help guide other readers to these wonderful books. Even if it's only a line or two, your reviews help readers discover the author's books so they can continue creating stories that you'll love. Log in to your favorite retailer and leave a review. Thank you.

Kathi S. Barton is an award-winning and bestselling author known for her steamy paranormal romances and unforgettable characters. A recipient of the prestigious Pinnacle Book Achievement Award, her books have topped the charts on Amazon and All Romance eBooks, earning her a loyal global readership.

Kathi lives in Nashport, Ohio, with her husband, Paul. When she's not crafting passionate love stories set in magical worlds, she enjoys camping, exploring local auctions, and attending county fairs, where Paul showcases his artwork and pottery. Her creative spark—fueled by a muse she describes as a cross between Jimmy Stewart and Hugh Jackman—brings her stories to vivid, heartfelt life.

Paranormal romance with plenty of heat is her favorite genre, and she loves connecting with her readers. Feel free to reach out—Kathi would love to hear from you.

Email: aaronskiss@gmail.com

Follow Kathi on her blog: http://kathisbartonauthor.blogspot.com/

www.ingramcontent.com/pod-product-compliance
Lightning Source LLC
LaVergne TN
LVHW090515110826
845146LV00003B/866

* 9 7 9 8 8 9 1 2 6 5 1 6 5 *